I contentedly giggling away, and then something happens. Miriam flips her long hair over her shoulder, and it's in slow motion. The sun bounces off the golden hues of her silky blonde strands. She smiles, and it radiates from within, igniting a warmth deep inside my chest. Her soulful eyes twinkle with a keen awareness.

So lovely. I've noticed there's an intelligence in those eyes she tries to mask. Perhaps that is what lures me in. Her secrets make me feel like she is the mystery I was born to unlock.

I stand there frozen, completely captivated. Breathless. Wondering how in the hell I am ever going to let her go, but knowing I must. Tonight we marry, and if I want to keep my sanity, I cannot let my heart wish for more than that. A ceremony. Not that she wants a real marriage, but if she did, it would not work. I am a vampire and she needs to stay human. Those two things do not mix.

WHAT ARE TASTY HUMANS SAYING ABOUT THE LIBRARIAN'S VAMPIRE ASSISTANT SERIES?

"A complex vampire mystery with laugh-out-loud moments and an utterly charming hero."

—*Sara, @HarlequinJunkie*

"I'm addicted to Michael and his merry band of dysfunctional vampires. I giggled my way through this book and thoroughly enjoyed myself."

—Leigh, Guilty Pleasures Book Reviews, on *The Librarian's Vampire Assistant, Book 2*

"I have a weakness for Mimi Jean's books. She must write with crack or something else equally addictive."

—Library Queens, on LVA

"[Michael Vanderhorst] is absolutely hilarious, with Mimi's awesome trademark one-liners that make you laugh out loud."

—Kathy, Ahmazing Book Faerie, on *The Librarian's Vampire Assistant*

"Just can't stop smirking! Reading anything by Mimi Jean Pamfiloff leaves me in a better mood for hours!"

—Tome Tender, on *The Librarian's Vampire Assistant, Book 2*

"This cozy vampire mystery is very different from what she has written before but is still very classic Mimi with all the surprise twists, turns, foul language, sassy women, and brooding men."

"It's a cozy mystery with a dash of paranormal that has humor, heart, and characters that you will fall in love with from the beginning."

"You will be hard pressed to put it down once you have started."

OTHER WORKS BY MIMI JEAN PAMFILOFF

COMING SOON!

My Pen is Huge (OHellNo, Book 5) ← WOW.
WOW. WOW. This cover.

The Boyfriend Collector, Part 2 ← I'm going to
need valium to write this.

THE ACCIDENTALLY YOURS SERIES

(Paranormal Romance/Humor)
Accidentally in Love with...a God? (Book 1)
Accidentally Married to...a Vampire? (Book 2)
Sun God Seeks...Surrogate? (Book 3)
Accidentally...Evil? (a Novella) (Book 3.5)
Vampires Need Not...Apply? (Book 4)
Accidentally...Cimil? (a Novella) (Book 4.5)
Accidentally...Over? (Series Finale) (Book 5)

THE FATE BOOK SERIES

(Standalones/New Adult Suspense/Humor)
Fate Book
Fate Book Two

THE FUGLY SERIES

(Standalones/Contemporary Romance)
Fugly
it's a fugly life

THE HAPPY PANTS SERIES

(Standalones/Romantic Comedy)
The Happy Pants Café (Prequel)

Tailored for Trouble (Book 1)
Leather Pants (Book 2)
Skinny Pants (Book 3)

IMMORTAL MATCHMAKERS, INC., SERIES

(Standalones/Paranormal/Humor)
The Immortal Matchmakers (Book 1)
Tommaso (Book 2)
God of Wine (Book 3)
The Goddess of Forgetfulness (Book 4)
Colel (Book 5) ← Serious book BUZzzz.

THE KING SERIES

(Dark Fantasy)
King's (Book 1)
King for a Day (Book 2)
King of Me (Book 3)
Mack (Book 4)
Ten Club (Series Finale→) OR NOT?

THE LIBRARIAN'S VAMPIRE ASSISTANT

(Standalones/Mystery/Humor)
The Librarian's Vampire Assistant (Book 1)
The Librarian's Vampire Assistant (Book 2)
The Librarian's Vampire Assistant (Book 3)
← YOU ARE HERE ☺

THE MERMEN TRILOGY

(Dark Fantasy)
Mermen (Part 1)
MerMadmen (Part 2)
MerCiless (Part 3)

THE LIBRARIAN'S VAMPIRE ASSISTANT, BOOK 3

MIMI JEAN PAMFILOFF

A Mimi Boutique Novel

Cover Design by Earthly Charms
Developmental Editing by Latoya Smith
Copyediting and Proof Reading by Pauline Nolet
Formatting by Paul Salvette

TO PIRATED BOOK LOVERS

"I'm not hurting anyone."
"I can't afford to buy books, so the author isn't losing money. I'd never buy them anyway."
"I don't think it's wrong. So many people do it."

As an author who is trying to support her family on this income, it's really difficult to come up with the right words to convey how damaging ebook piracy is to me personally, to my fellow authors, and to the industry. (Remember, publishers HAVE to make money, too. We want them to. They have employees with families like anyone else. They create jobs and pay taxes in our communities. Businesses need to be healthy because when they're not, people get laid off and lose things like their homes.)

As for the individual author, well, I just can't imagine anyone being okay with working for four months at their job on a presentation and then their boss says, "Hey, I'm not going to pay you because I can't afford it. Also, I know that I used the presentation and you did the work and slaved over it, but I never had the money to pay for it in the first place, so you really haven't lost any money. Either way, you weren't going to get paid."

Hell no would you put up with that!

Bottom line is we all have a right to decide how

we're compensated for our work and time. Strangers, the public, and book pirate sites don't have the right to decide for us. It's okay to have an opinion about what you're willing to pay for my books or to have a political view about access to books, but that doesn't give anyone the right to decide for the author or artist.

As for these sites that claim they're not doing anything wrong? The sites pirated book lovers go to and think they're not hurting anyone? We all KNOW THEY ARE.

What sort of person or organization would put up a website that uses stolen work (or encourages its users to share stolen work) in order to make money for themselves, either through website traffic or direct sales? **Haven't you ever wondered?**

Putting up thousands of pirated books onto a website or creating those anonymous ebook file-sharing sites takes time and resources. Quite a lot, actually.

So who are these people? Do you think they're decent, ethical people with good intentions? Why do they set up camp anonymously in countries where they can't easily be touched? And the money they make from advertising every time you go to their website, or through selling stolen work, **what are they using it for? The answer is you don't know.** They could be terrorists, organized criminals, or just greedy bastards. But one thing we DO know is that **THEY ARE CRIMINALS** who don't care about you, your family, or me and mine. **And their**

intentions can't be good.

And every time YOU illegally share or download a book, YOU ARE BREAKING the law and HELPING these people BREAK THE LAW. You are helping them get paid for my stolen work via web-traffic and ad impressions.

Meanwhile, people like me, who work to support a family and children, are left wondering why anyone would condone this.

So please, please ask yourself who YOU are HELPING when you support ebook piracy, and then ask yourself who you are HURTING.

And for those who legally purchased/borrowed/obtained my work from a reputable retailer (not sure, just ask me!) muchas thank yous! You rock.

DEDICATION

To chocolate chips.

Not only do you make cookies better, but you get vampires drunk. And you make really wonderful snowman eyeballs on my Christmas treats.

THE LIBRARIAN'S
VAMPIRE ASSISTANT
BOOK THREE

CHAPTER ONE

"Can you repeat that? You're a *what*?" Miriam's eyes widen as she maintains a calm façade from the comfort of her brown leather couch. We are surrounded by thousands of books, three stories high, all overlooking her spacious living room, and I cannot help feeling judged by each and every one of them. Not that books actually judge anyone, but they simply have that conceited vibe. It is what I love about them.

"I think you heard me," I respond. "I am standing two feet away."

"Michael," Miriam frowns with a huff, "you can't be serious."

"I'm afraid I am, Miriam. I am a vampire." I stand over her, my chin held high as I stare down at her lopsided dirty-blonde bun, which I have come to adore along with her shabby sweaters, though today she has on gray sweats and a T-shirt. Now that the cat—or shall I say bat?—is out of the cave, I'm guessing things will finally start making sense to her.

Which things? you wonder.

Given the abundance of unusual events that

occur when in the presence of vampires, I wouldn't know where to begin. Perhaps she wonders how I always manage to catch her when she falls from the ladder in her library even if I'm halfway across the room. *Clumsy little thing.* Or maybe she has always sensed something is a little off with the company I keep. Vampires can be quite eccentric.

I focus on Miriam's oval face, waiting for her reaction. She is a smart, inquisitive woman and will have many questions, I'm sure.

Suddenly, her cheeks turn from a rosy pink to a pasty white.

Uh-oh. I think she is going to scream. Perhaps I have been too indelicate with the delivery of my shocking news. It is not every day that someone in your employ tells you they are a four-hundred-year-old, fanged killing machine—a fact I have somehow managed to keep from her, my boss. Of course, merely looking at me, one only sees what I show them: a twenty-year-old college student living on the budget of a part-time assistant librarian. I would also add that I am six one with dark brown eyes and hair and have been told I am a shockingly handsome man. I mean, handsome vampire.

And handsome a-hole. Dammit, you fool. Why did you have to blurt out the truth to Miriam like that? I watch in horror as her face changes colors like a mood ring, landing on a fiery red. She is either about to have a panic attack or turn into a ripe tomato.

Excellent work, you bastard. Upsetting my precious librarian is the last thing I need right now, because while the past month has been hell on Earth—my maker being murdered, me being forced to take leadership of two large territories (including this one here in hellishly sunny Arizona), and being falsely accused of running a vampire blood farm—nothing compares to the news I just received from Lula, my right hand, two minutes ago. It is the reason I decided to come clean with Miriam. I had no other choice given how impossible it will be to conceal the truth any longer. A war is coming, and I have been tapped to lead.

But how can the generals name me, of all people, the vampire king? Yes, I am a second-generation vampire, which makes me stronger than most. I am also a seasoned soldier and trained assassin who once fought to bring an end to the violent, tribal existence of my kind. But that was long, long ago, and since then I have been many different things: a hunter, an English professor, a barber, a detective, and a bioengineer, just to name a few.

And now you are an assistant librarian who may or may not be incredibly attracted to his boss. All right, yes, yes. I cannot stay away from her. I want to bed her in the worst kind of way. And my need to protect her body, mind, and soul, with all that I am, gnaws at my immortal heart, day and night, though I cannot say why.

Why her?

Many females have crossed my path over four centuries, yet she is the one I am drawn to. She is the reason I can say without shame that I am not meant to be a king. I am meant to be by her accident-prone side, playing with her delicious books.

Ah…such a tantalizing collection. I salivate at the thought of touching her first editions. Not only does Miriam have her private collection right here in her home, but she also owns a library near downtown Phoenix, twenty minutes away. *A woman with so many books is too sexy for words.* In short, after all that I have done for my kind, they cannot rob me of the only thing I have ever truly wanted: a librarian to call home.

I wince as she doubles over on her brown leather couch. *Poor woman. Be strong. We will get through this together.* I will keep her safe from not only her extreme clumsiness, but from the violence of my world.

I lean down and rest my hand on her back. "I realize this is a lot to take in, but you must know I will do everything in…" My voice fades as I note her jiggling shoulders.

What the devil? I scowl down at my blonde little librarian. "Miriam, do not laugh. This is not a joke. I'm a vampire, over four centuries old."

She sits upright, gives me a serious look, and then falls forward again, unable to stop laughing.

I shake my head and cross my arms over my

chest. I'm wearing jeans, Converse, and a Captain America T-shirt today. *Ridiculous outfit.* But it is vampire law that one must dress according to the age they look and according to their profession in the human world—a sort of camouflage to avoid drawing attention. However, at the moment, I feel silly trying to have a serious conversation with a superhero logo on my chest. What am I? Twelve? I am not much for shopping, but I will have to stop grabbing T-shirts from the bargain bin at Target.

"Miriam, listen to me. We have to leave here. It is no longer safe for me, which means it is perilous for you."

Wiping the tears from the delicate skin of her cheeks, Miriam rights herself again. Her cupid-bow lips twitch with a grin. "I always knew you could make me laugh, but..." she lets out a happy sigh, "I really needed a good chuckle." She hops to her feet, places her hands on my shoulders, and beams up at me. "Thank you."

I cannot believe she thinks this is a joke. What we are facing could make a grown vampire weep. Not me, of course. Because I am Michael Vanderhorst. Son of Cluentius Boethius, a first-generation vampire, which makes me a sort of prince.

"Michael?" Miriam snaps her fingers in front of my face. "Are you even listening to me?"

Nope. I am too busy fuming. "Miriam, I appreciate how outlandish my confession seems, but I swear on my life that I really am a vam—"

"Bup!" She holds up a small hand. "No need to continue the comedy act."

Everyone knows she is special to me, which means she's about to become the target of every savage vampire around the globe. Ergo, Miriam Murphy has just become my biggest liability in winning this war. *Nowhere near close to comedy.*

A twitch of dread pulses deep in my stomach. *Dammit, man. Stop it. You've fought in the Great Vampire War. You've slayed thousands of deadly, evil vampires. You are Michael Vanderhorst!* I win at everything I do, despite the obstacles. It is what makes me a legend, feared by the masses.

I straighten my back and apply my sternest expression. "Miriam, you know I consider myself a gentleman, and gentlemen do not go around frightening women or children. We protect them." I lean down and stare deeply into her wide brown eyes. "I am a vampire. I drink blood. Sure, I also enjoy strong coffee and vegetarian cuisine with blistering hot chili peppers because it makes me feel alive, but I still require blood to live. Just like your ex-boyfriend Jeremy."

Miriam's smile melts away.

Good. I've finally gotten through to her. *Wait… Uh-oh. Maybe not?*

Her plump little lips flatten, and she balls her tiny hands into tight fists. Rage shoots from her eyes. "That wasn't funny, Michael. You know how much I miss Jeremy. How-how could you make a joke out of that?"

Oh, Jesus… Miriam's ex and his boss got involved in the blood-farm scandal and were murdered by whoever was behind it all. They wanted to cover their tracks. Up until now, she was unaware that both men were vampires and that Jeremy was not a good man.

Someday I will tell her the entire story. "I'm sorry I mentioned Jeremy. Truly. But we have no time to play gam—"

"No!" She stands and points an angry finger in my face. "You do not get to talk about him. You do not get to use his name for a gag."

How can she think so little of me?

"Miriam, I apologize, but you must trust me when I say he was *not* who you think. I am *not* who you think." I begin opening my mouth to flash a bit of fang.

"Get. Out," she barks, angrier than I've ever seen her.

"Miriam, I—"

"You heard me. Get *out*! You promised to never lie to me again. You swore the bullshit would stop, yet here you are, doing it again. You don't understand what it's like to lose the people you love, Michael. I lost my parents. I lost my boyfriend. I almost lost my library! So how," she throws her hands in the air, "could you possibly think asking me to lose my sanity would make me feel better?"

I hang my head and sigh with remorse. Though she accuses me of being insensitive, it's quite the opposite. I hear her loud and clear: One more loss, one more heartbreaking ordeal, and she will break. She still mourns the loss of her parents in an accident last year, and Jeremy is never far from her thoughts. She's been threatened, attacked, and kidnapped more than once these past few weeks, all because of Jeremy's illicit dealings, which she knows nothing about. Still, if I truly mean what I say about protecting her mind, body, and soul with everything I have, then I cannot push her further. Vampires and the violence to come with this war must remain in the shadows as long as possible.

I bob my head and offer my most remorseful expression—furrowed brows and puppy-dog eyes. "You're right. I'm sorry. Sometimes I get carried away." I smack my forehead. "Stupid college student, yanno."

She narrows her eyes. "You need to leave."

"Going." I raise my palms in surrender. "But please don't stay mad. I really was trying to make you feel better—I know how much you love those vampire romances and—"

She holds up a hand to stop me.

I nod in compliance. "See you at the library."

I leave her house, knowing she will be safe for the moment. Her Southwestern-style mansion has a basement, a vault, and two separate wings of rare and priceless books. Her state-of-the-art security system will keep out any intruders—at least long enough for me to show up and assist her, should she call for help, which she will if she feels afraid. That is the mystery between us. I need her. She needs me. Neither understands why or is ready to confront it. Simply put, our bond is a mystery.

Speaking of...what will I do when she leaves the house? Because, despite modern myths, my kind *does* walk in the sun. We hate it—especially in this sunny hellhole called Arizona—but we do it. Therefore, she is in danger twenty-four seven from my enemies.

I slide into my black rental SUV and shove the key in the ignition. *I'd better figure something out fast.* She'll be leaving for work in a few hours. *I will have to return later and follow her to the library.*

I crank the engine, and it roars to life with a knock and a sputter. *That's odd.* I put it in drive and head for the gate. The moment I exit Miriam's property, the SUV begins to chug. One block away, the thing dies.

Well, crap.

CHAPTER TWO

"I'm sorry, dude, but we're all out of midsize and large vehicles. We got four conventions going on this week, so…yeah. But I have your lucky car. Cool, right?" The rental lot attendant points outside to my nemesis, but I refuse to look. The vehicle offends everything I hold dear about my masculinity.

Instead, I glare at the young hippy man. "Surely you must have something else. Something bigger."

"Nope."

Dammit. This electric car is like a rash that won't go away. Over the past month, I somehow keep getting stuck with it. *I really should buy a vehicle.* I just never seem to have the time, and when I first arrived in Arizona last month, I hadn't planned on staying. That's all changed now.

Finally, I turn my head and eye the compact blue monstrosity sitting all alone in the lot like the uncoordinated child no one wants on their rugby team. *The thing looks like a child's toy.* But not the charming kind you reminisce about decades later, such as a rock you push with a stick or pair of knucklebones—my personal favorite as a child. All right. Fine. Toys of the 1600s truly sucked. *And so does this car.*

"Sorry, man," says the clerk. "Everything coming in today is reserved. You can try the lot down the road, but I called them earlier for another customer. They were booked up, too."

Dammit. I could start calling around, but there's no time to lose. We're in the middle of a crisis. Our enemies are about to attack because they believe we should all return to the old ways, when humans were openly preyed upon and covens lived in a state of constant war over hunting grounds.

Ridiculous.

Our enemies are crusty-minded, power-hungry delusionals. Humans are no longer the easy game of two thousand years ago. Today, they have weapons and technology. They have armies. If vampires were found out, we'd be no match, and taking our council members prisoner will not change the truth.

Oh, did I fail to mention that part?

Yes, all one hundred and forty-four council members from around the world have been taken. It is a page right out of the vampire warfare playbook. Cut off the head of the snake. If the snake grows another, keep on chopping. If the snake hides its head, cut off the snake's arms and legs until it screams for mercy.

All right, snakes do not have appendages, but you get the point. You also get why I am not so excited about being the interim leader. Our enemies will look for any weakness to exploit. Everyone I care for will be a target. Lula, my right hand, who is currently manning—or womanning?—my territory of Ohio, is strong and fast. She can take care of herself. But people like Miriam? Or my young vampire assistant, Viviana, here in Phoenix? They will be sitting ducks.

What's an ancient, powerful, but unwilling-to-be-king to do? He must reestablish order by returning our council members to their rightful places. Then they will lead the effort to defeat these ridiculous vampire degenerates who risk exposing us all.

So where are our enemies hiding?

How big is their army?

Where have the council members been taken?

I do not know, but I intend to find out.

Mystery! Mystery! Mystery! My inner-vampire child jumps up and down with sadistic delight. Even now, under such dire circumstances, it cannot resist the thrill of playing detective.

First things first, however, I must assemble a team of guards for myself and those around me. After that, I will arrange a secure way for the generals around the world to discuss a defense plan while I find out where our missing council members are.

Point is, I do *not* have time to hunt down another car, and I wouldn't dare send anyone on a frivolous errand for me. King or not, leader of two territories or not, my job is to protect my people, not to be pampered by them.

I hold out my hand. "Give me the blue scrotum." The ancient man inside me groans in agony. "But I want an SUV or something larger the moment it becomes available. You hear me?"

"We're booked for the week, so…" The clerk gives me a look, and I know what he wants. He is into guys, and though I could never fault him for wanting a piece of this impressive slice of manliness, I am not what he's after. I recently paid him a few thousand dollars—no questions asked—to drive the blue turd cake. He and I have a similar build, so I used him as a double when I was being followed. To match our appearances, I cut his hair like mine, which did wonders for his love life. Happy to help, of course. *A man must always look his best.* However, he's been bothering me for a trim ever since. I am an excellent barber, but I have no time for such things.

Yes, but you cannot be stuck with that blue cheesedoodle.

I sigh with defeat. "Find me scissors, but I want my SUV back."

He smiles. "I will move your name to the top of the list."

When I arrive to my office an hour and a half later, my assistant, Viviana, is waiting inside with a delicious triple-nonfat-latte in her hand. With all the running around this morning, including returning to Miriam's home and secretly ensuring she got to work safely, I'm just as anxious for my caffeine fix as I am to hear an update. Also, I need to get back to the library as soon as possible to check on things. I hate leaving Miriam alone, but I must deal with this situation.

"How did your hunt for guards go?" I eagerly snatch my coffee from Viviana's hand. She worked through the night, compiling a list of qualified warriors to guard us. Each territory—aka "society" or coven—is already supposed to have its own security; however, the prior guards all worked for the former leader, who had his hand in every scheme possible, including the blood farm I mentioned. When I took over, I immediately kicked them all to the coffin. I do not tolerate traitors. That is not to say I am against breaking vampire law. I've been known to bend a rule or two. Or a few hundred.

The disappointment in her green eyes is immediate.

"What is the matter?" I ask, noting that her brown bob looks freshly coiffed, and she is wearing a stylish blue dress—formfitting and low cut. She is an attractive woman to be sure, but my librarian, with her bottle-cap reading glasses and sloppy manner of dress, is the only female who has ever caught my eye. It goes without saying that I have bedded women when the need arose; though, work has been my constant lover. As for Viviana, she is a loyal assistant and smart as a whip, which is why it's odd she went home to bathe and change her clothes. We have urgent work to do.

"I can't get you any guards." She sighs.

"Why not?"

"Because every capable fighter has been called to active duty by our generals."

"Well, they are going to have to give some up. I cannot act as king without protection." After all, it was the generals who determined I should lead. "Get General Otto on the phone." His real name is Dieter Ottovordemgentshcen-blah-blah-blah. It's rude to call a general by his first name, but no one has the time to actually say his entire last name, even if we're all immortal.

"Yes, sir." Viviana scrambles to her desk, which sits in the middle of the room, surrounded by filing cabinets. We have no windows or natural light in this two-story brick building since sunshine bothers us, but the pale yellow walls and fake plants help to improve the cheeriness factor.

"Send the call to my office." I take the stairs and close the door behind me. I have only been in power a few short weeks, so there are no personal items. Just a solid mahogany desk and a leather chair.

I go for the phone and press the blinking red button. "Otto?"

"Vanderhorst, I'm sure you're looking for a full military assessment, but I have yet to reach all of the other generals."

Not good. There are a total of five hundred and eighty-two societies around the world, all broken into twelve geographical regions. Each region has a council of twelve, and one of those members sits on our international council. The military is structured exactly the same but with generals. Otto leads Europe but is the head of the more powerful international group.

"And which regions aren't reporting in?" This could be a clue as to who is working with the enemy.

"I'm still waiting for a full head count, but I am told several have gone dark."

Very bad. If we don't have support from the majority of territories, including their generals and armies, we will be in serious trouble.

"Have you tried reaching the individual society leaders from those areas? They might know something."

"We have, but no one is saying much. They don't know who is friend or foe and refuse to answer questions until they are certain they're talking to the good guys."

Crap. This is exactly what I feared. Without the leadership councils in place, each territory will put up its walls and treat everyone else with distrust. It's what our enemies want: to use our natural suspicion of other vampire societies against us.

"If we do not stick together, we have no hope of

winning," I say, thinking about how this is starting to feel all too familiar. During the Great War, when the vampires of the old world began attacking territories that wished to exist peacefully with each other, they tried to prevent us from banding together. The old rule would attack a family and make it look like it came from another coven on our side. The retaliation was immediate and brutal, sparking a coven war before anyone heard the facts. For this reason, the laws of today require that all justice be handed down by a society leader or by their region's council. Of course, vampires aren't big on rules. Everyone knows that.

"They're taking another page from the Great War's playbook," I say.

"We have to make sure this doesn't happen."

Ya don't say... "Get the word out: Going forward I will administer all trials. If anyone is suspected of a crime, they are to be arrested and brought to me." I feel mighty kingly all of a sudden. "No one is to harm a hair on a fellow vampire's head until I have seen to a proper trial. To do so will be an act of treason." I can only hope that my reputation, the one that earned me the nickname of the Executioner during the Great War, will prevent anyone from defying me.

"Sir, I see where you're heading with this, but how will you have the time?"

"I won't." There is no possible way to help win a war, protect my people, and act as vampire sheriff for the entire planet. "This is why we must hurry to find our real leaders and free them."

"You really think they're still alive?"

I do not know who is spearheading this rebellion, but I do know who is running their army: Alex. He fought by my side during the Great War. He watched my back. He was a good friend. *Until he turned on us all for reasons I do not understand.* But when it comes to war, I taught Alex everything he knows, and it would be foolish to kill prisoners, especially high-ranking ones. They can be tortured and used for valuable information. They can be traded for POWs later on.

"Unless the other side is being run by a group of nut monkeys," I say, "then our leaders are safe. I simply have to locate them. As for you and all available generals, please start devising scenarios of defense. We could be hit one region at a time or all at once." My money is on the former, considering our enemy's army is probably only a thousand or two strong. Ours is closer to eight if all able-bodied fighters have been called in. However, Alex's army has been pumped up with second-generation vampire blood, which means they are ten times stronger than your average vampire. That had been the whole purpose of the blood farm we discovered in the massive catacombs beneath Miriam's library a few weeks ago. At first I thought that the people behind it were after money—selling immortality to wealthy and elite humans. Then I learned the truth:

They captured my maker, Clive, and drained him to death, using his blood to make five hundred more vampires, whom they milked like cows.

Those bastards will pay for what they did to Clive. He was a good, good man. He fought to make this world a better place for humans and vampires alike. Symbiosis versus hunter and prey.

Anyway, that blood, as strong as my own, was given to our enemy's army. So while the other side might not have our numbers, they will make up for it in strength and speed.

"If I were them," I say, "I would attack each region, territory by territory."

"But where will they hit first?" Otto asks.

"It's anyone's guess. South America is a big place with a large army. Take them out first, and the rest of the world will be a piece of cake."

"We'll get back to you with strategic options, but, Vanderhorst, I think you need to come here to Blackpool and meet with some of the other generals. Otherwise, they might decide that 'every vampire for himself' is the best course of action."

Having us all hop on planes and gather at our UK headquarters would be a disaster. "If we assemble in one place, we could be hit again, and without our generals, we'd certainly lose. I will give the alternatives some thought. In the meantime, I need men here. I have no guards."

"I will assign twenty soldiers to you. Another ten can be spared for your office of…" he snickers, "the Arizona Society of Sunshine Love."

Yes. Yes. I know the name is ridiculous. However, I did not make it up. The previous nincompoop who led this territory chose it, and once a society is established as a legal entity in the human world, we cannot change it. The less attention we draw, the better. Our society is registered as some sort of conservation group, dedicated to creating public awareness about the health benefits of sunshine. The founder likely intended it as a joke, but it makes our members come off as idiots. If I had my druthers, I'd rename us something with purpose, such as the Arizona Society of People Against Tiny Stupid Cars.

"Thank you, but as acting ruler, I will decide the best place to station these men," I finally say.

"You're going to guard that librarian, aren't you?" Otto asks.

News travels fast in vampire land, and given recent events, which I won't go into right now, everyone knows about her. All the more reason for around-the-clock security.

"Someone has to protect her," I say. "So it is either them or me. And given I've been drafted into the leadership position, I think my time will be better spent elsewhere." Such as dressing up in a disguise to infiltrate the enemy's prison in order to free the council. *Once I find the location.*

"I mean this respectfully, Vanderhorst, but the optics are bad. Powerful families are giving up their personal guards to reinforce our armies."

"Surely protecting one human, who can be used as leverage against me, is not an issue."

"Your subjects will not see it that way," Otto throws back. "As we speak, our men and women are preparing to give their lives. They take their loyalty and sacrifice very seriously. It will be seen as an insult to make them babysit your plaything."

Plaything? Miriam is no toy. Yes, I wish things were different, but they are not. Still, our connection is almost sacred. It is a bond unlike anything I've ever heard of. That said, I do understand Otto's point. If I were ordered to leave my family to be in the army, and then asked to risk my life for a leader's human pet—not that Miriam is—I would not be pleased. Unfortunately, I cannot change reality.

"The people are simply going to have to choose," I say. "Protect those who are important to me, or find another king."

"You are the only person our societies will trust and follow. You'd turn your back on them for one little human?"

"She is little in size, but her personality is quite large and impressive, I assure you. Nevertheless, she is no match for a vampire, and I won't turn my back on those who are under my protection. Not her, not Lula, not even you, Otto. And I don't even like you." He's a general, but he is practically a baby—a little over a hundred years old. He served in WWI before he was turned, which means he has some experience with warfare, but not much. Still, he looks like he's sixteen and walks around like he's seen it all, done it all. Cocky to the core.

"No one likes me," he retorts. "My masculinity threatens them."

Right. Sure...

He continues, "Vanderhorst, I could understand if this human was your queen—your mate for eternity—but she's not. She's just a librarian."

How dare he! If we were speaking face-to-face right now, I would rip out his throat. Books are sacred and librarians are the keepers of books, which makes them sacred, too.

"I would give my life for Miriam, just as I would give it to help our people," I point out.

"That doesn't mean our army will feel the same, and if you force the matter, you risk fragmenting our societies."

Dammit, he has a point. As important as Miriam is, asking a bunch of strangers to protect her with their lives is a nonstarter. Vampires are notoriously loyal, but it's always to their families and societies first, then to their regions. But never to a human unless that human is their blood—a wife or child from their pre-vampire days.

"This might sound outlandish, but have you considered marrying her?" Otto asks.

"Making her into a vampire? No. I will not." She deserves to live her life in peace, to grow old and have a family. She once told me herself, during a hypothetical discussion, that life was precious because of its finality. She said becoming immortal—like the character in that Fanged Love vampire series she adores—would take away everything she cherishes about being alive. I.e., being alive. *Can't argue there. Being dead, frozen in time, is a grind.*

"I didn't say you had to make her immortal," Otto clarifies. "She just needs to be your wife. Given how traditional vampires are, they will feel it's their duty to protect their queen, too."

"You mean perform the wedding ceremony with a human?" I turn to sit on my desk, the phone gripped tightly in my palm. I think Otto is onto something. In my people's eyes, this would make her an extension of myself. Male vampires are fiercely protective of their women. The only drawback is that humans are not permitted to know about us.

I wonder if they will let it slide. At the moment, there are nastier fish to steam. *Or fillet? Or…darn, I do not recall what happens to less desirable fish, but the focus will be on other things.*

"Send the men," I command. "Tell them she and I will be wed by the time they arrive."

"Very good, sir. I will be in touch later. And please be careful."

"You, as well." I end the call, and a sour wave of dread mixes with excitement in my stomach. *Miriam. Mine?* Deep down inside, I know we are not destined to be together. She is and must always remain human. But that other part of me, the vampire, the possessive male who wants her, is elated by the thought.

The question is, which side will win? Because once I make her mine, I know I won't ever want to let her go.

CHAPTER THREE

"Michael, are you out of your putrid, crusty old head?" Lula's shrill voice pours through the phone. "How the hell do you plan on marrying Miriam without her knowing?"

"I am Michael Vanderhorst. I specialize at all things impossible."

"Uh, no. You're a giant dumbass. A vampire wedding is a big deal. When we say 'until death do us part,' it actually means *forever*. It's why so few vampires marry."

Lula is correct; most vampires opt for cohabitation. Many do not believe in everlasting love at all. Personally, I'm still unsure if such a thing exists. True love, soul mates, and eternal bonds take on an entirely different meaning when you don't have an expiration date. Then again, what do I know? Up until a few weeks ago, I barely had an emotion, let alone experienced love. Loyalty, yes. A sense of duty, certainly. Needs, such as hunger or arousal, all the time.

But love?

It was why I always considered myself a lone wolf, having little contact with the members of my society and spending most of my time focused on work. Four centuries and nine professions—not counting this temporary appointment as king—and not once did I consider taking a wife. Part of me has always wondered if being the Executioner damaged me beyond repair. I killed so many that I had to stop feeling emotions in order to stay sane. Then Miriam came along.

"I truly am out of options, Lula. Options and time."

"Is this the part where you ask for my help?" She takes a snippy tone with me.

"You know me so well." I put my cell on speaker and take a seat at my desk.

"Yeah, which is why it's a miracle I'm still talking to you."

Lula and I have a long history, consisting mostly of me underestimating her, her saving my ass. What can I say? I am trying to change my ways, but this vampire was not built in a day.

"Yes, it is a miracle," I reply. "And I shall be forever in your debt for all that you do, which really buys you nothing since we are family and you already have my loyalty." Clive was her maker, too, but she is only two hundred years old—half my age. Nevertheless, she has been tapped by the generals to lead my two territories of Ohio and Arizona while I attend to bigger matters.

She huffs. "Just tell me what you want. But if it has the word *librarian* or *Miriam* in it, the answer is no."

"Actually, I was hoping you could come back to Phoenix. Run Cincinnati from here."

"Why? My house is here. My life and my society are here. Also, it's not five hundred degrees outside."

"You are now in charge of both territories in my absence, and Phoenix requires more attention. It's like the Wild West here. They have no regard for tradition."

"You mean they don't show up to boring society meetings, or their ass-kissing doesn't meet your standards?"

"Neither," I snarl. "Attendance is fine, and my ass is adequately adored. I am referring to the fact that they are apt to follow whoever spins a better yarn about being the strongest or most powerful. *You* can teach them the true meaning of duty, loyalty, and bravery."

"Ugh. Speaking of ass-kissing… *Ding, ding, ding!* You want my help duping your librarian into marrying you, don't you?"

"No…" I reply shamefacedly. "Okay, perhaps yes. But I also need assistance finding the council members. We may have to fly off at a moment's notice and rescue them."

"I can fly from here. And I'm not helping you trick Miriam into marriage."

"Why the hell not?" I growl.

"Because I kind of like her. It wouldn't feel right."

Well, there's a change. Lula used to be jealous of my feelings for Miriam, primarily because Clive made Lula for me—a fact I recently learned after his demise. Since then, Lula and I had a night together and agreed that we are not meant to be forever companions. She is my best friend, and I am her leader, but nothing more. Still, vampires hate sharing. That includes sharing your best friend with another woman.

"I am pleased to hear you've let go of any animosity for Miriam, Lula. Very pleased. However, if you truly care for her, you know we must do something to protect her. The entire vampire world knows of my relationship with her."

"Don't you think it's weird that they know about this relationship and she doesn't? Just tell her the truth."

"I tried that, and she did not handle it well. I do not want to break the poor woman, given how much she's been through. Besides, telling her won't change anything. She must still be protected. She must still be my queen. And she will say no to both whether she believes vampires are real or not."

"I see your point, Mikey, but I think you're misjudging her, and she has a right to know about the full extent of the danger."

I hate being called Mikey but let it slide. I have bigger fish to net or whatever. "The truth will terrify her. And she's already made it clear she will have nothing to do with me if I broach the vampire subject again."

"Oh, you're such a pussy."

"Am not." I am the Executioner. Or was. I fear nothing except tiny blue cars.

"Are too."

"I cannot help it if I feel the need to shelter her from all this," I argue.

"I'm calling Miriam. Then you'll see you're just being an overprotective machoron."

"What the devil is a machoron?"

"You. A macho moron."

"Harhar. Leave Miriam alone," I command.

"She's going to wonder why a group of scary, heavily armed, deadly vampires are following her around. Have you thought of that?"

"Of course not. I am man, and we resolve one problem at a time, but we do it well."

"*Pfft!* I'll call you back."

"Lula, no. You are to come to Phoenix and help me—"

The call ends, and I stare at my phone, smoke billowing from my ears. "Dammit! Why must she always defy me?"

"Sir?" Viviana and her perfect brown bob pop through the cracked door. "I heard yelling. Anything I can help with?"

"Why is your kind always so...so stubborn! I am the king. I am not to be disobeyed!"

"Okay, Joffrey." She rolls her green eyes.

"Huh?"

"Nothing."

"No. You were about to say something. Out with it," I demand.

"I don't think I should. You'll get angry. And we all know bad things happen when the Executioner loses his cool."

"Nothing bad will happen! And I'm already uncool—I mean coolless. Or...whatever. Just speak your mind."

She inhales sharply. "Fine. I think the problem isn't us women, sir. It's men like you who refuse to see the truth or listen, even when a woman is screaming the facts right in your face, all because the idea or thought didn't come from you. But deep in your heart, you know women are right ninety-nine percent of the time."

"No one is right that often," I grumble. "Not even me. And I'm always right."

"But *we* are. It's because *the ladies* don't give an opinion or take a position until we have the facts. You men always run off, swinging your willies, trying to pass off opinion and hypothesis as facts."

"We do not."

"If you say so, sir." She looks away, finding a sudden interest in the plain white wall.

I narrow my eyes at Viviana. If I did not need and like her so much, I would fire her for insolence. And for insulting my willy-swinging ways.

The cell on my desk vibrates, and I grab it. It's Lula. "Hello?"

"You were right. I started to mention the whole vampire thing, and Miriam flew off the handle. Said she will murder the next person who mentions, quote, 'stupid vampires.'"

I look at Viviana, knowing she heard every word with her vampire ears. "See you here in the morning," I say to Lula and end the call. Vindication is mine. I would do a victory lap and swing my manhood about the room, but I simply do not have the time. Instead, I look at Viviana and cock a brow. "What were you saying about men being wrong all the time?"

She shrugs. "Even a broken clock is right twice a day." She strolls out, leaving me there, stewing in my Converse high-tops. I detest sneakers as much as I detest being robbed of a win. *And I won that conversation.*

I draw a steady breath and exhale. Though there are many distractions in my life, I must remain focused on the tasks at hand:

1. Figure out possible locations where the council members are being held.
2. Devise a secret wedding with my librarian before the guards arrive. (Note: include a reason for why a pack of ruthless, deadly vampires are following her around.)
3. Stay alive.

Wait. Scratch that.

3. Keep *everyone* alive.
4. Help win war.

My stomach grumbles, and I realize I haven't had enough to eat lately. I'm still recovering from the trials and tribulations of the last month.

My mouth waters as I imagine scarfing down a plate of baked soy cheese, vegan enchiladas with habanero salsa, and a side of fire-roasted chilies. *Mmmm…Mexican.*

I tap the side of my cheek. *Or maybe I should have a Mexican for lunch.* I hear a few cartel members were recently released from prison and are now up for grabs on our menu. The tastiest people are always the murderers, rapists, and pedophiles, all of whom are melt-in-your-mouth delicious. The badder they are, the more spicy and flavorful they become.

Just this morning, for example, I had vampire *serial* for breakfast. This particular male murdered at least twelve people and enjoyed torturing kittens, which gave his blood that extra punch of savory aromatics. Innocent humans, on the other hand, taste like eating an old leather shoe. *But a good gangster? Delicious.*

My mind suddenly drifts to something else I crave. Something I ache for but refuse to give in to. Something I want to taste and feel and lick from head to toe before I plunge my—

No. No librarian! Stay on task, man. I cannot

afford to be distracted by sexual fantasies at a time like this, no matter how powerful the urge, an urge that grows stronger by the day.

Enchiladas. Flaming hot enchiladas. I need them now! But for how much longer will spicy food and vampire serial keep my primal needs at bay?

CHAPTER FOUR

After my fiery meal and having ample time to digest the tasks at hand, I now have a solid grasp on my plan of attack with Miriam.

Possible locations for the council members is another matter, but I have Viviana checking which societies have been quiet lately. She came up with the brilliant idea of checking who did not RSVP to the council's ball. It is an annual event, and all five hundred and eighty-two society leaders are invited. There's even a Sexiest Dead Man Alive Award. Yes, Viviana nominated me. Yes, I am in the lead. Yes, I am furious about it. I am Michael Vanderhorst, most powerful vampire alive. My stunning looks are inconsequential. In any case, there is a strong possibility that our enemies were too distracted by their activities to reply: *Hey, Vlad. I know we're going to try to overthrow our government and enslave the human race this summer, but want to attend the ball anyway? Sounds like fun.* Not a likely scenario.

Next, Viviana and Lula will start making calls to all of the societies who did not RSVP. During my years working for Clive as a detective at his agency, I found that most vampires are not very good liars, but we are excellent lie detectors. Everyone knows this; therefore, those who refuse to have a conversation with us will be suspect.

We will weed out the players. We will find the council members. We will restore order.

As for Miriam, I must get to work quickly. We have about twenty-four hours to complete the ceremony. And I know just how to get it done.

∿ ∿

"Charades? Tomorrow night?" Seated behind the desk in her office, Miriam quirks one blonde brow. As owner of this privately funded library, founded by her recently deceased parents, it is her job to curate and fill four stories of shelves, though her shoestring budget hasn't allowed her to hire any full-time help. She depends mostly on me and the goodness of the community. It amazes me how much people adore her, though. They come and go, borrow and return on time, and watch over this enormous collection of books as if it were their own. Perhaps that is what drew me here on that fateful morning when I was visiting from out of town, grieving for my maker, who was murdered for his blood. I came looking for answers and wandered into Miriam's library while looking for a place to clear my head.

Seems like a lifetime ago, though it has only been about a month.

I look around her cluttered office toward the back of the building on the first floor. Books of all sizes and genres cover every surface, stacked ten or twelve high. My fingertips tingle with the need to dust or organize or…something. Anything.

"Yes," I say. "Charades. I'm having a small get-together at my new apartment and thought it would be fun." I still haven't found the apartment I speak of, but I will. My current "college student" accommodations are horrendous, which is why I recently told Miriam that I inherited a small amount of money from an estranged uncle. This way she doesn't suspect where the money for better housing came from.

Miriam looks down at a gardening book about bees cradled in her hands. She loves books as much as she loves this library and reads everything before putting it on her shelves. I revere her dedication.

"I'm not sure I'm up for it, Michael," she says, a muted sadness in her tone. "I have a lot of work to do and reading to catch up on."

I know she is still upset about this morning's conversation about vampires, and I want to say the perfect words to smooth things over. She's been through a lot lately and I am only adding to her stress. "My dear woman, I realize it has been a treacherous past few—"

"Stop. You know I hate it when you talk like you're a character from a BBC period piece."

Ah yes. While I look and dress the part of a

twenty-year-old, I always forget to sound it.

I clear my throat and prepare to interject lots of umms and yannos. "Yeah, sorry. Uh…I've been practicing for a play, so I'm trying to sound all old 'n stuff. We're doing *Hamilton* in my drama class."

"You? You're taking acting?"

No. I have all the drama one man can stomach. "I joined an off-campus club," I lie and shrug like a sloppy youth from this day and age. "To meet girls, yanno?" Sounds like a plausible excuse for a twenty-year-old, right?

I wonder if Miriam will get jealous. Hmmm…

"You actually disgust me sometimes. I can't believe I let you work here." Miriam's lips flatten.

"What?" I respond defensively. "We all know the women of the theater aren't exactly beauty queens." At least, not during the 1600s. Missing teeth, bad breath, a ruddy complexion from drink. I mentally shudder with revulsion. "But hey, it's not their fault they're hideous. But what they lack in looks, they make up for in personality."

Miriam crinkles her nose like she's just smelled bad cheese. "Sometimes, I think you're the smartest person I've ever met, wise beyond your years, and then you say things like that."

I don't get it. I just tried to tell her that I am willing to date ugly women for their intellect. Doesn't that make me a good guy, even if I just made it all up? *I simply do not understand the females of this time.*

I have no choice but to pass my comments off as a joke. I laugh and point a finger at her. "Had you going, didn't I?"

Miriam frowns. She didn't like it as a joke either.

"Sorry. Bad form. But I'd really appreciate it if you'd come tomorrow. Yanno?"

"Why? So I can meet all of the *ugly drama club girls* you're blessing with your presence?"

Let it go, woman. Just let it go. "No girls. Just Lula and Viviana—my, uh…she's my acting coach." Viviana was turned in her thirties so she looks ten years older than me. Miriam's already met Lula and believes her to be my ex-girlfriend. "Oh, and a bunch of the guys are coming, too. They're all practicing for parts in a theatrical version of *Rambo*, so expect lots of fake guns, tight shirts, and camo."

Miriam slowly nods. "You run with an interesting crowd."

"Just wait until they start kneeling and calling you their queen."

"Why would they do that?" Miriam's brows scrunch together.

Great question. *Give me a moment to think of another plausible excuse.* "After the *Rambo* thing is cast, there's, uh…uh…" *Crap.* The only stories I remember with queens are *Cinderella, Snow White,* and… "They're trying out for *Game of Thrones.* Extras."

"Isn't that over?"

How the hell would I know? Vampires don't watch those silly types of shows. The disappointing finales just make us angry.

"I guess they're bringing it back." I wink like I know something she doesn't. "Anyway, I'd really appreciate it if you'd come to my get-together. It wouldn't be the same without you." I offer Miriam my most alluring look: hooded lids, a charming smile, flexing jaw to show off the angles. I know she feels drawn to me, even if she does not wish to admit it.

She stares into my bedroom eyes for a long moment. *Come on. Say yes. Say yes...* The air starts to hum between us, and I feel her emotions. It's like I can taste them in the air.

Fascinating.

"Fine." She rolls her eyes. "I'll go. But only for an hour."

Perfect. By my calculations, I only need twenty minutes to perform the ceremony. "I'll text you the address tonight."

"Great." She forces a smile. I know something else is on her mind. Come to think of it, something is on mine, as well. A loose thread.

"Um...Miriam?"

"Yeah?"

"Remember how you were going to rent out several rooms in your house?" She mentioned doing it a few weeks ago, after the city threatened to shut down her library if she didn't retrofit the building, a million-dollar expense she couldn't afford. Turned out that some land developers were after her property. Also turned out they were working for Jeremy and our enemies. As I mentioned, beneath all those floors of books are massive, naturally formed catacombs, the perfect place to hide illicit vampire activities, such as that blood farm. One of the access points is a block over, but Miriam's library sits directly over another big cavern that they had wanted to use to expand their operations.

Thankfully, these land developers are no longer. I put a stop to the scheme, and her building is fine; however, I need to be sure she's not still worried about money.

"How could I forget?" she replies.

"You're not going through with that anymore, are you?"

This time, it's Miriam who's shrugging. "I don't know… I was thinking about interviewing a few candidates."

"But why?" The hairs on the back of my neck stand straight up, looking for a fight. Yes, even my hairs are fighters. I am quite manly like that. "Everything's settled with the city. You don't have to do any retrofitting. I checked myself."

"It's a huge relief; I can't even begin to tell you. But I live in that enormous house all by myself."

"If it's a question of feeling protected, I can assure you that your alarm system is adequate and—"

"No. It's not about that. I've been blessed in so many ways, and there's tons of space I don't use. I could give a good person a home. Maybe a student like yourself." Miriam had actually suggested I take a room myself, and I can't lie; I was tempted. What man wouldn't want to be closer to such a beautiful woman and catch a glimpse of her walking around in a nightgown? *Or accidentally dropping her towel in the kitchen after she has just showered, her skin glistening with drops of water, her shoulders and delicate neck completely exposed, begging for a nibble?* I mentally sigh with pleasure. *Dare to dream.* But it would have been impossible to hide what I am if we lived under the same roof. *And dream gone.*

"No. I do not approve of another man living with you," I exclaim, quickly realizing I've overstepped my bounds. "I mean…" I swallow my overly protective male pride. It feels like I'm choking on a giant furry sock filled with thumbtacks. "It's not wise to let complete strangers in your home. You have millions of dollars in rare books just lying around. Some are priceless."

"I'm going to screen everyone, and the most valuable items are locked in the vault."

I shake my head. "I just don't like it." And I really want to get inside that vault. Just for a peek. She says all of her rarest first editions are down there. *I want to touch them.*

She chuckles bitterly. "You don't have to like it. I'm thirty years old and don't need yours or anyone's approval."

"Thirty? When was your birthday?" And how do I not know her damned birthday?

"Today, actually."

Oh, God. And I did not get her anything. I didn't even slay an enemy or bury any bodies in the desert for her today—the sort of thing that tells a woman how much you truly care. *I must try harder. I want to be a good husband to her.*

I quickly pull myself back. I am going to be her husband in title only. It's a means to an end and nothing more. After this war is over, I'll have our marriage annulled. It's never been done, but I am the ruler. I can make it a law. I *will* make it a law.

My selfish inner-male bucks in protest. He doesn't ever want to let her go. "Well, then...happy birthday. Let me take you out tonight to celebrate since I didn't get you anything." *And since I have to follow you home anyway.*

"Let me guess? You want to take me to happy hour at the Beer Hut?"

The local college hangout down the street? As if I'd be caught dead in any establishment that has the word *hut* in it. Beer Hut, Sunglass Hut, Pizza Hut. Not very vampire. Still, I must keep up my "college dude" appearances. Now more than ever, so she doesn't suspect what is going to happen tomorrow or that she will be in an apartment filled with deadly immortal soldiers. *Not to mention followed around by ten of them.*

"What's wrong with the Beer Hut?" I ask. "They have two-for-one chicken wings tonight and Miller Light on tap for fifty cents." The thought of drinking such swill nauseates me. A good Bordeaux or perhaps a fine single-malt scotch could hit the spot. "But if that's not your thing, we could go somewhere fancier. The Cheesecake Factory, perhaps?" I truly have no idea where humans like to dine these days, but I see these Cheesecake places all over. They must be popular.

"Thanks, but no. I have plans already."

What! "With whom?"

"None of your business, Michael. Now if you don't mind, I have a mountain of paperwork and two books to get through."

Her eyes flash to the pile of paperbacks on her desk. Peeking out from beneath a copy of Dr. Phil's latest book is something I immediately recognize: *Fangless in Seattle.*

Is book three out already? One of our council members, the infamously unpleasant Mr. Nice, happens to be obsessed with the Fanged Love series, though I cannot say why. Seems like a campy vampire parody to me—capes, coffins, and moats. Not that I've read it. *More than once.* Nice learned about the books one night when he came into Miriam's library with me. She happens to be a huge fan, too, though I also do not understand why, considering her aversion to even discussing vampires. Either way, I had needed to occupy Mr. Nice for a few moments and handed him the first book. He's been holding the author hostage ever since, demanding more books.

I hope the writer has figured out a way to get free from Nice's basement. He is among our enemy's prisoners, so who knows what's become of the poor authoress. I'd send someone to check, but no one knows where the one-thousand-six-hundred-year-old Mr. Nice actually lives. Even if they did, who would be brave enough to enter his dwelling?

Eesh... I bet his home looks like the Munsters' junkyard. That, and he is quite possibly the deadliest, scariest vampire on the planet. *And this coming from a man called the Executioner.*

I bow my head toward Miriam. "Enjoy your books. And I hope you have a happy birthday. With your *friend.*" I will be following her tonight, of course. She has no idea of the dangers lurking in the shadows. I mean, other dangers lurking besides me. "I'll send you the details for my housewarming party later." I turn to leave.

"Michael."

A few feet from the door, I stop and face her desk again.

"I don't think it's such a good idea." Her eyes shift away, and she fidgets with a paperclip she's found on her messy desk.

"What's not a good idea?"

"You. Me. Socializing like that. I don't want you to get the wrong impression. I'm your boss.

You—you're just a kid."

Kid. Very funny. Here is where my vampire senses come in handy. Her pulse is rapid and her cheeks are flushed. The sweet floral aroma of her delicate skin fills the room with the rising heat of her body. *She is lying.* Which means she thinks socializing is a very, *very* good idea.

So why would she tell me otherwise?

I give Miriam a look so *she* knows that *I* know she is lying. "I assure you my '*impression*' of us is entirely accurate." With my mouth closed, I involuntarily swipe my tongue over my aching fangs. My twins want her.

She stares at my lips, and I hear her already rapid heartbeat accelerate into a furious gallop. I catch a whiff of her body letting off potent pheromones—an involuntary human response when one desires the attention of a potential sexual partner.

I smirk with male pride. This is the second time today that I have been right. *Winning!* "See you later, *boss*. And happy birthday." I leave her to her lusty vampire book, knowing it is my face she'll be seeing when she reads the tantalizing love scenes.

Such a shame she doesn't want to let a real vampire into her bed.

CHAPTER FIVE

That night I do what I do best: lurk in the shadows, waiting for Miriam's "friend" to arrive. By midnight I am certain she either made it all up or this mystery person is a no-show. Either way, I find myself at odds, stuck between knowing I should give her privacy and wanting to make up a ridiculous excuse as to why I happened to be in the neighborhood. Miriam is a bright young woman, loved by many. She shouldn't have to be alone on her birthday. Except, perhaps, if she wants to be. Not everyone is a fan of turning a year older. I, myself, could not care less. Once you reach the age that no human is meant to live to, it becomes an endless blur.

Just after midnight, I hear some modern music playing in her living room—Nat King Cole, I think—and opt for leaving Miriam alone. I do not want to fight with her on such an important day.

Our wedding day...

Excitement courses through me, all the way down to my groin. *She will be my wife.* Mine to please in bed, to hold, to sniff. *Her fruity shampoo does smell amazing.*

Suddenly, a twitch of guilt ticks in my stomach.

What the devil am I doing? I should be off finding our council members, not fantasizing about sniffing Miriam's hair and making her my real wife. But here I am, watching over my librarian like a hawk, fearing something might happen to her. All because of my choice to be a part of her life. If my plan to wed her tomorrow doesn't go as I hope, and I fail to obtain the protection of my soldiers for her, I do *not* know what I'll do.

Turn my back on everyone who is counting on me? All for her?

Could I live with myself if we lost the war?

It would mean that everyone I care for will die. Humans, including small children, will be hunted like farmed trout. Or chickens. Or whichever docile creatures are raised for their meat these days. Millions of innocent, non-spicy, flavorless humans will perish, simply to satisfy the whims of the power-hungry evil few. Then, after the initial slaughter, when humans figure out that the myth of bloodthirsty vampires isn't a myth at all—except for the "blood-only diet" and "no walking in sunlight" part—humans will get their acts together and wipe us all out.

This war is a zero-sum game. How do our enemies not see this? How do they not understand that we should live in anonymous cooperation with the species we once were? Personally, I'm proud to cull the dregs of human society from the herd.

I eat.

They are safer.

It's a win-win.

The only drawback is having to pretend to be human. *Don't forget driving the tiny blue shit stain. God, I hate that thing.*

On the way to my studio (my soon to be ex-studio), I pick up some Chinese from a place around the corner that serves the hottest vegetarian chow mein on the face of the planet. It literally makes my balls hurt, but I enjoy anything that reminds me I am still alive.

"What a day." I come through the front door and go straight to my miniscule kitchen table, which is literally two feet from everything in my *casa de cucarachas.* I have seen coffins larger than this dump. And prettier, too. The walls are a grungy white, the furniture is falling apart, and the shag carpet is more of a quilt made from remnants sewn together.

I cannot wait to move out.

I take a seat at the table and look at my phone. A text from Lula informs me she'll be here at first light. Viviana says she's still working on getting the full list of non-RSVPers, but should have it soon. By morning, we can begin making calls and weeding out suspects. All we need is one good lead. One crumb to follow. The rest will be a question of persistence and good old-fashioned detective work.

I pop open my carton of hellfire noodles and get to work with my chopsticks while I scroll through emails. *Now there's some positive news.* Viviana has forwarded a list of five executive suites available for immediate rental. They're the kind that come fully furnished and you can stay in for a night or rent for months—a glorified extended-stay hotel, really.

I move through them with a quick flick of the finger. *Ouch. Ten thousand a month?* I can afford them, but the college student I'm supposed to be cannot. It won't help with keeping up appearances. Sadly, I'm out of time, so I have to choose something.

I pick the least fancy option with good lighting in the parking garage and plenty of exits—four on every floor. Planning for retreat is just as important as planning for victory.

I text Viviana and tell her to book the place tonight and make sure it's ready in the morning, stocked with beverages and snacks. The human kind. I want Miriam to believe this gathering is your basic drama-nerd party.

Unexpectedly, I feel my bones vibrate with trepidation. I know something terrible is coming, but this is what separates a seasoned warrior from the dead ones. I've made my share of mistakes, and they have taught me one important lesson: not to panic. When I was younger, I would jump in with both feet toward any threat, too confident in myself to see that determination alone doesn't win battles.

A knock at my door startles me from my thinking mode. I stand and listen to what's on the other side. Not a hint of a breath or a heartbeat. Either the person has just dropped dead or it's another vampire.

Fuck. I rarely use this word or even think it, but now seems appropriate. I am unprepared for an attack, and there is only one exit in this dump: a small window in the bathroom, hardly large enough for a skinny cat.

I could punch through the wall or—

"Vanderhorsthsssth!"

"Mr. Nice?" I jerk open the door and find a dirty, gangly man in tattered lace.

"*Sank zi* gods!" Nice rushes in, nearly knocking me over. "Do you have any Nice T?" He goes straight to my small fridge and finds the bag of fresh blood. Before I can warn him that the donor is unknown, he's punctured the film and is sucking like a baby. "Num, num, num…"

He must be starving. Because Nice is about as eccentric as they come—from his very strange accent to his rule about only dining on blood from people whose names start with the letter T (aka "Nice T") to the nightmare of lace and leather he wears on his tall wiry frame. With his long black hair, he literally looks like he walked off the set of an '80s goth video, though I think most would agree that his fashion is the least frightening thing about him.

He's old.

He's powerful.

He'll rip your head off with the flick of a pinky

if he doesn't get his way. *All the more surprising that he doesn't care whose blood he's drinking.*

"I must *habe* more!" Nice tosses the empty pouch on the floor.

"That was my last bag, sir, but allow me to call my assistant and find out who's on the menu."

"No!" He points a finger in my face. "No one can know I'm here. *Zi* spies are everywhere, Vanderhorsthsssth." His dark eyes dart wildly from side to side.

I was so startled by his presence that for a moment the war thing slipped my mind. "Hold on. Where did you come from? Who took you? How did you escape?"

Nice drags his fist across his mouth, wiping away a few dribbles of blood. His long black hair is matted with dirt and his leather pants are more brown than black—their true color. I know this because Mr. Nice is not a brown pants type of man. He'd consider it showing weakness to wear anything the color of excrement.

"They took me while I was at a private screening of *Fanged Love.* They put something over my head so I wouldn't know the location."

"Dear Jesus. They're making the book into a movie?" I shake my head. "Sorry. That's frightening, but not important. Where do you *think* they took you?"

"It was cold, dark, and one of the men smelled like curry."

"Indian curry?"

"No. More like coconut with lemon grass."

"Thailand." A good choice for hiding out. Very inconspicuous. Not many vampires like Thailand, given the heat.

"Impossible. I was only in the air for six hours, seven maximum."

Hmm…interesting. My inner Sherlock scratches his chin and lights his pipe. "Where did they take you from?"

"I cannot say."

"You do not recall where you went to the movies?" I ask.

"I recall, but I cannot say. My turf is confidential. A vampire of my age and standing can never be too careful."

"Nice, sir, with all due respect, we are at war. Every detail you provide will assist us in winning."

"Ugh…the Nice is tired of winning. For once it would be nice to lose. Such a refreshment, no?"

I frown with confusion. "No. Not in my experience."

"Ah. But have you ever lost?" He holds up a long skinny index finger to punctuate his point.

"No."

"Then how would you know?"

I feel like we are going down a rabbit hole. For crazy vampire rabbits. "I suppose I do not, but let us assume that I can enjoy the experience of losing some other time. This particular war is one I feel strongly about winning."

"Party pooper," he grumbles.

"All the way. Now, if you don't mind, would you give me an approximate location for your abduction?"

"Nice enjoys the nightlife—*zi* jazz, *zi* blues, *zi essanem* clubs, you know."

"*Zi essanem* clubs?" I have no clue what that is, and to this day, I still cannot figure out his accent. According to the rumor mill, Nice—short for Nicephorus—was a Byzantine general in the 800s, but that does not explain his manner of speech. *It's like he has multiple personalities from different countries and they're all trying to speak at the same time.*

"*Zi essanem.* You know. With *zi* whips and chains." He snaps an invisible whip in the air.

"Oh, S and M." But those sorts of establishments can be found in many big cities. "Mr. Nice, I promise to never reveal the whereabouts of your hometown."

"I *weel* tell you if you go out and bring back Nice a juicy T-bone. I am very hungry."

"You want steak?"

"I am a vampire, silly. I want to dine on someone named T-Bone."

All righty... Perhaps he was hit in the head during his escape. "Sure. No problem," I say to placate him.

"New Orleans. That is my home."

Of course. Where else would a crazy old vampire live? "So…six or seven hours by plane leaves a lot of options."

"I think we headed east."

I narrow my eyes. Why the hell didn't he just say so? "Did they take you to the UK?"

"I believe so. Did I not say this already?"

"No. No, you did not. Any other details you might want to share, such as the place they held you or how you escaped and made it back to Phoenix?"

"There were other council members there. We were questioned and thrown in a pit with our ankles and wrists chained together. It was cold and dark."

A pit? It seems as though our enemies are looking for a Great War do-over, copying many strategies. There were once large dirt pits near our headquarters in Blackpool, England, a leftover from the Great War. We had run out of vampire-proof prison cells and had to opt for throwing our enemies into what were essentially deep wells. With one's arms and legs bound, it was impossible to climb out. I do not know what covers these pits today, but I assumed they were capped and built over.

"How did you escape?" I repeat.

"*Diss* is the part I do not understand. Someone helped me. I could not see them and they did not speak. They also had their scent masked with Jovan Musk for men."

Jovan Musk. A trick Clive taught me when I worked as a detective. Drakkar Noir works well, too.

One dab and no vampire will be able to catch your scent due to the potent smell and ensuing headache. So who else did Clive teach this trick to?

There is only one person I can think of. Only one person who was close to Clive like I was: Alex.

But why would he help Nice escape?

"So this person got you out and then what?" I ask.

"They put me back on a plane. We landed and they transported me in a van and tossed me outside your building."

"They brought you directly to me? None of this makes sense. Unless it is a message." Could Alex possibly be working as a double spy? Could he have delivered Nice so I would figure out where the council members were taken?

Alex would know I'd find meaning in Jovan Musk. He'd know the pits would ring a bell, too. In fact, it was he and I who coined the phrase "it's the pits," i.e., the worst possible situation to be in. Somehow, it caught on and is still a common phrase used today.

"Then I will travel to Blackpool and attempt to verify the council members' location before we make a move." However, I will need to travel quietly because I agree with Nice; spies are everywhere and the chances of getting captured will be extremely high.

"You do whatever you like, but I want my T-Bone and a long nap. Nice needs to hibernate for a few days."

I bow my head. "Of course, sir. I will get your meal at once, but I'm afraid there's little time for naps. We have much to prepare."

"Ah, *pfft*!" Nice swipes his hand through the air. "Wars come and go."

"That is precisely the point. We need to make it *go a*way."

"Yes, but how long until another group comes and challenges us?"

"Hopefully never if we're running things the right way," I reply.

"Ha. Ha. Hahahahaha…" He laughs and then turns deadly serious. "Get me my food or I will disembowel you through your belly button."

"You do realize I am the king, and—"

"Now, Vanderhorsthsssth!" He holds up his grubby pinky with a razor-sharp fingernail.

"Yes, sir." I turn to leave before I am left staring at my own intestines. That is not the last thing I wish to see before dusting—a term used to describe the way we die. We simply turn into a cloud of gray dust.

"By the way," he says, "what happened to your little librarian, eh? I hope *zi* Fanged Love wedding is still a go."

Dear God. Not even war or being kidnapped has made him forget. Long story short, I may have told him that Miriam is my soul mate. In truth, I do not know what she is to me, but there were questions being raised about how involved she was in the blood farm, given her ex-boyfriend's participation. I'll point out that vampire justice is not the same as the human sort. One must only look guilty to be convicted. So, in order to keep her out of hot water, I had to claim her as my own and vouch for her. As part of this claiming, I also had to promise to turn her and then marry her in exchange for leniency from the council. Of course, much has happened since then, but Nice is still expecting a big Fanged Love–themed wedding according to the book—lots of red lace and horse carriages involved. Blech.

Thankfully, now I've got an out...

I clear my throat, wanting to approach the subject carefully. "Unfortunately, Mr. Nice, sir, I have run into a small problem. Given this war and the fact we may be attacked at any moment, I am afraid a lavish, well-publicized wedding is out of the question. We would all be sitting ducks, and I cannot put my bride-to-be in such danger. Therefore, I have decided to elope with her in a secret ceremony." *So secret, even she's unaware.*

"Oh..." He claps wildly. "*Diss* is very romantic! I will have to be there, your witness to *zi* Fanged Love of real life."

Oh no. No, no, no. Nice cannot be there. He will terrify poor Miriam, not to mention say something to tip her off.

"I do not think it is a good idea for you to leave the apartment," I say. "Not when there are naps to be had and spies to hide from."

"Do not be silly. I wouldn't dream of missing it. When is the big day?"

This upcoming evening. "Next week. I think perhaps Monday." I will simply have to risk disappointing him.

"Very nice. Ah, see! I made *zi* joke there. Now off with you, Vanderhorsthsssth. I must have my rest, and I am getting vangry."

"Vangry? As in, very angry?" I ask.

"As in vampire hangry." He shakes a finger at me. "You really should keep up with the cool slang, Vanderhorsthsssth, especially with your cover story."

"I will hit the internet as soon as I return," I say to placate him.

"I would never hit that. So dirty." He plunks down on my disgusting brown couch.

I blink, grateful for the opportunity to leave. "Be right back with your juicy T-Bone."

I head out to the parking lot and call Viviana. She is the keeper of the list, the "menu," of humans approved for killing. The call goes into voicemail, so I text her…

> Me: *911! Need menu. Must look like he's possibly named "T-Bone."*
>
> Viviana: *T-Bone?*
>
> Me: *Don't ask.*
>
> Viviana: *I'm actually afraid to. Get back soon with menu options.*

Next, I text Lula, who should be on a plane and en route.

> Me: *Nice was freed and brought to my studio. Possibly Alex is behind it? Sounds like council is in the pits. Call when you land. Go straight to my new apartment.*

> Lula: *Nice is there? Right now? And of course the council members are sad. They're prisoners.*

> Me: *Yes. He's here. And I meant the pits near UK HQ. We need to confirm before POT is formed.*

> Lula: *Now you're growing weed? You do know that'll make you fat.*

> Me: *Stop it.*

> Lula: *Make me. I'm thirty thousand feet in the air, and last time I checked, you can't fly.*

I groan. She's trying my patience.

> Me: *POT = Plan of Tackle*

> Lula: *You really need to stop trying to be cool. It's plan of attack, Mikey. GWI = get with it, for you old farts*

I may be old, but I am no fart. I am more of a fine wine or a classic novel filled with whimsy and sophistication.

> Me: *Just be prepared for dangerous mission after wedding.*

This time, Lula has nothing to say. I suspect she is unhappy about the ceremony. Like I said, vampires do not like sharing.

I decide to let it go and simply trust in my bond with Lula—a new thing for me. Up until recently, I trusted no one even if they'd already proven themselves. Alex's descent has not helped my reluctance, but Lula's loyalty and willingness to place herself in harm's way—for me, for our family, and for our kind—has taught me a thing or two. If I ever doubt anyone again, it will not be her.

CHAPTER SIX

Around six in the morning, Nice has cocooned himself in my narrow closet, sleeping upright with his arms crossed over his chest. Very disturbing. Lula is just arriving to my new apartment, freshening up, and will meet me at the library around noon to plan for tonight and for our trip to the UK. Otto has texted and informed me that my private guard unit is on the way, arriving this evening. I am showered and dressed in my white "When I think about books, I touch my shelf" T-shirt, plus jeans, and boots. The shirt is for Miriam. I think today of all days requires as much distraction as possible if I am to pull off the vampire wedding ceremony without her knowledge.

I just pray today goes well. Already I'm starting off with a dead body in the trunk of my blue nightmare. *They really must make the storage larger for these cars.* I could barely fit the poor bastard "T-Bone" inside. Had to get creative with the direction of his limbs.

I glance at my watch. *Jesus. I'm already late.* I hit the road and head straight for Miriam's place, stopping along the way for a triple latte and a hot tea for her. I need a reason to be at her house so early.

When I arrive, I punch in the code to her gate and drive through. She's just coming out the front door as I pull up. The home is an impressive example of modern Southwest architecture with nods toward the adobe style—big windows, wooden beams, and a flat square roof, but the cactus gardens and wrought-iron doors have more of a modern upscale flair.

"Well, good morning," I say through the passenger side window I have left open. Don't want my car smelling of leftovers.

"Michael, what are you doing here?"

"Was in the neighborhood. Thought I'd bring you some caffeine." I hold up the tea.

She narrows her eyes, and her plump little lips pucker. I am hypnotized. There's nothing more enticing than a feisty librarian—brains and gumption. My shaft stirs in my jeans.

"Just happen to be in the neighborhood? You promised you wouldn't lie any more, Michael." Miriam crosses her arms over her narrow chest. I try not to notice the bit of cleavage showing along the neckline of her pink blouse. The shirt is too big on her and sags a bit in the front. Her iron gray skirt is just as unflattering, hitting her below the knees. A pair of black sensible flats and reading glasses hanging from her neck complete the nerdist look.

For the life of me, I cannot comprehend why

she feels the need to hide herself away under all those frumpy clothes. I've seen this woman in a tight evening dress, so I know she has quite the little body going on.

"Fine," I say, "I am here because I wanted to apologize again about yesterday. I went too far."

"You said that already, but then you had Lula call and keep the prank going. Why would you do that?"

"It was a little miscommunication. Won't happen again." I offer her my sincerest please-forgive-me smile.

"No more vampire talk? Promise?"

I bob my head. "Promise."

She reaches for the handle of my door and hops in.

Oh crap. I freeze. I had not intended to drive her in. I merely thought to say hi, drop off her tea, and follow her to the library.

"Well?" She grabs her tea. "Are we going or not?"

"Uh, sure…just keep the windows down. I think the last person who used this car was transporting roadkill." *Or dead bodies nicknamed after steak.*

"What happened to that SUV you were using?" she asks.

"It's in the shop. This is the only loaner they had."

"Ah. Nice shirt, by the way." She smirks. She

knows I wore it just for her.

I hit the accelerator, and we're on our way. I try to keep my cool, but I'm watching everything and everyone around us.

"So, how was your birthday?" I ask, wondering if the no-more-lies policy applies to herself.

"Great."

"Where did you and your friend go?" I inquire.

"Why do you ask?"

She's avoiding the question, but not lying.

I shrug. "No reason. I guess I'm always on the lookout for good eats. Yanno?"

"Mmmm…" She nods but doesn't offer more. I decide to drop it.

"So, you all ready for your party tonight?" she asks.

Not even close. Before this day is done, she and I will be man and wife. She will be my queen.

My body starts to hum with hard tension, knowing how badly I desire to consummate the marriage.

"Yeah." I swallow down a dry lump. "My new apartment is great." Not that I've seen it yet.

"Must be nice having a little extra money."

As I said, she thinks I inherited some cash from an uncle. Really, I just used money from my checking account. Back in Cincinnati, I have a very different cover and a large publicly declared inheritance. In Phoenix, such a cover wouldn't be possible. Not if I wished to remain working for

Miriam. A vampire's cover story must make sense, and wealthy people typically don't take minimum-wage jobs. Really, that is how she and I met. I wandered into her library, and she thought I was a college student applying for a part-time job. I ended up playing along, and the rest is history.

"Absolutely," I say. "That reminds me... I need to take some time off. Just three days. Four tops."

"Where are you going?"

To investigate some dark, scary pits in an attempt to save the world. "Well, you know how my uncle died recently? He left me his collection of books. I need to go through his storage locker to see what's what," I lie.

"You're going to *sell* his books?" She sounds appalled, like I'm auctioning off his children on eBay.

"I might keep a few, but I have to assess what he's got first."

"And since when did you become an appraiser?" she asks, sounding suspicious.

Since I was born before the United States of America and before the age of television, so I've had lots of time to read and learn. My private collection of books back in Cincinnati is very respectable, though it pales in comparison to Miriam's. Her family began building the collection several generations ago, and her parents spent millions acquiring more. *My kind of people. I would have liked to meet them.*

"I'll figure it out," I say.

"I can go with you if you want? I mean, I am

looking to expand my collection and—"

"Thanks, but then there'd be no one to watch your library." Oh no. She cannot come. It will be far too dangerous. Plus, I do not want to call any attention to my activities.

"That's actually not true. I put an ad in with the university for two part-time assistants."

No. There can only be one assistant librarian: me. "I don't like it."

"Sorry?" she snaps.

There I go again, overstepping. She does not understand my apprehension related to strangers. They could be spies. Also, Miriam is a danger magnet. Case in point, look who's working for her.

"I meant," I clear my throat, "I don't like it…when I'm not trained properly for a job. Very frustrating. I assume your new assistants will feel the same?"

"Actually, the two applicants already have experience working in the university library, which has the same software. I think they're more than qualified to help out."

"Oh." We pull up to a red light, and I stare straight ahead. I'm torn. I *would* feel more at ease having her remain close to me, especially at such a perilous time, but we are not really going to look at books. This little investigatory trip could be dangerous.

Although… I scratch my chin. *I do happen to have a storage locker just north of London.* It contains a few items left over from my parents' estate—glassware, several paintings, and some furniture. I believe there are few old trunks filled with old books. *Likely turned to dust by now.* Nevertheless, they could serve as my "uncle's collection."

"Hey, if you don't want me to go, just say so. I was only trying to help," Miriam says. "And green light."

I glance at the stoplight. "Oops. Daydreaming." I hit the accelerator, but when I glance at Miriam, her eyes are a little glossy and the corners of her sweet little mouth are turned down. I wonder if she simply doesn't want to be alone.

Who cares? She wants to be with me.

My ego does a little tap dance and then takes a bow. It cannot resist a damsel in distress.

"On second thought," I say, "I love the idea. I know my uncle mentioned some rare finds. Would really hate to give them up without knowing what they are."

"Really?" Miriam smiles, and it tickles my cold heart.

"Just as long as you let me pay for the plane tickets and hotel," I say.

"I couldn't. You're just a student. I wouldn't want you wasting your money on me."

"I plan to pay for the trip with some of the book sales. Also, did I mention my uncle lived near London, but his lawyer, for some really weird reason, is near Blackpool up north? So we'll have to fly there first to pick up some paperwork. The cost will be fairly high."

"Oh. He lived in the UK? In that case…I'll let you buy the tickets, but if we don't find something good, I'll pay you back."

Miriam owns millions of dollars of books and lives in a mansion located in the most exclusive neighborhood in the Phoenix area, but her parents left her no cash, and she refuses to sell any of her books. In short, whatever cash she gets goes towards paying living expenses, property taxes, and running the library. Part of me loves how she gives everything to her passion. The other part of me wants very badly to take her shopping and spoil her a little. It's what a man should do for his wife—

Stop. Get a hold of yourself. She is not really going to be your wife. She'll only be mine in the eyes of the world's most powerful creatures. *Doesn't make it real. Nope. Not at all…*

"So when do we leave?" she asks.

"Tomorrow or the day after. I'm trying to get there before someone else gets to his things—some second or third cousins were upset that I got it all," I lie as an excuse to mask the urgency. I loathe having to make up so much phony bullcrap, but I've said it before and I'll say it again; I am a man of integrity, but I am also a vampire. We break rules when we need to. All part of the fun when you live a double life.

"Wow," she says. "I didn't realize you were leaving so soon. I mean, I do have a passport, but—"

"I wish it could wait a few weeks, but you know how greedy cousins are…" As we're talking, I realize that I'm going to have to bring a few guards with me. There is no possible way I can keep my honeymoon—I mean investigative trip—low profile if she comes along. Also, we will have to leave her alone at some point while Lula and I do our thing near Blackpool. I can explain Lula's presence, but the guards? Why would anyone bring members of their drama club with them to another country to inspect some books? Hmmm… On second thought, she really should stay here at home.

"No problem. I'll make it work," Miriam says. "I'm actually super excited. With everything that's happened, I haven't taken any time off for myself. I need this. I need a little distraction." She sighs. "Yeah. This sounds perfect. Thank you, Michael. I don't know how you do it, but you always seem to come to my rescue."

I am a man, and men love to feel important and needed. No shame in that. However, this response is unusual for an independent woman such as Miriam.

"Not to be nosey or anything, but is everything all right?" I ask.

"As good as can be expected, considering I was attacked, almost murdered, you had to kill two guys for me, and we were kidnapped."

Oh. That. The kidnapping was actually the council taking us into custody. It happened just a few weeks ago when I was accused of running that blood farm. Given the location, the council assumed Miriam was in on it, too. Long story short, Miriam was cleared, and I was set free after Lula outed Alex as the true mastermind. We also figured out what the blood farm was for. As for Miriam, she was returned home and told I belonged to some crazy cult who was behind it all. She and I haven't spoken of the event since, but I know it's been on her mind.

It also sounds like she's just now coming to grips with the fact that I have killed two men for her. Both were hired by the land developer who's now dead. Again, that whole episode is water under the bridge except in Miriam's fragile human heart. She feels guilty about what I've done in the name of keeping her safe.

If only I could tell her the truth. I have killed thousands, and while I won't claim it doesn't haunt me, adding a few murderous bastards to the list won't change a thing. To the contrary, it gives me pleasure putting my lethal skills to good use.

"If there's anything I can do, any questions you have or thoughts you want to share, I'm here for you, Miriam."

"I-I just want to know if *you're* okay."

"Me?" I am tormented beyond words. I cannot begin to think of what will happen if I fail to restore order. But *my* fear is *my* burden to carry, and I will do it alone, as I have for over four hundred years. Simply put, it is what men like me do. We battle demons. We stay strong. There is no other purpose for a man like me to exist. "I'm great."

"But you killed two people. Doesn't bother you, even if you did it to save my life?"

I know what she wants me to say. If I'm a normal non-psychopathic human, it should bother me.

I turn right, down the main thoroughfare, and encounter morning traffic. "I talked to a therapist, and I'm okay with it. Those men would have killed you, so I did what I had to. I'd do it again in a heartbeat." *If I had one.* Plus, they were tasty, so it was a win-win all around. The only downside was digging graves in the heat-infested desert.

Miriam nods stoically. "There you go again, sounding like a calm, rational man who's seen it all."

I don't want her to catch on, so it's time to sprinkle in some age-appropriate nuggets. "Well, I haven't seen as much as you. So. Old."

"Hey now!" She slaps my arm. "I'm not that old."

"Says the woman who is now thirty. Does it hurt to be so ancient?" I try not to smile, but it doesn't work.

"Very funny, Michael."

She's quiet all of a sudden, and when I glance her way, I notice she is studying my face. Actually, no. She is ogling me—pupils wide and receptive, a hungry look on her face. The shocking part is she doesn't look away or try to hide it. No. She wants me to know she's liking what she sees.

Dear God, what is happening between us?

I reluctantly put my eyes back on the road, and the car fills with tension. It's raw. It's sexual. *I am so turned on right now.* My manhood begins to stir once more.

No. No, sir. You shall not stand and salute the woman. We have a war to win. And something tells me I will need all the energy I can muster. But remember when I said that Miriam is my biggest weakness? I was wrong. My weakness is the spark between us.

Forget spark. Whatever this is, it's turning into a bonfire. And I do not know how long I will be able to keep my hands off her.

CHAPTER SEVEN

After trying to stay clear of Miriam all morning, for the sake of my pants and the children who come to the library, Lula makes her appearance around noon, an hour before my shift ends. As always, she's wearing an eccentric tribute to her independence as a woman—a skintight yellow leotard with yellow flats. Her blonde hair is braided in pigtails with matching yellow ribbons.

"Are you a dancer in Duck Lake—the ballet where the swan rejects go to die?" I try not to laugh.

"Okay, Mr. 'I touch my shelves.'" She rolls her eyes. "Where the hell do you buy all of your crap T-shirts from, anyway? The Dumb Fucker Store? Oh, wait! Don't tell me." Lula snaps her fingers. "You go to the Old Navy outlet. The real one. Because you're older than the navy. And the invention of ships, for that matter."

"Wrong answer. I went to your favorite boutique, The Immortal Frigid Spinster."

"That was a terrible comeback." She sticks her finger down her throat. "You're losing your touch, Mikeypoo."

"I've missed you." I wrap my arms around her

five-foot-four body and give Lula a squeeze.

"Eeeek. Careful there, mister. Don't want people getting the impression that I like you or something."

I let go of my trusty sidekick and beam down at her spunky face. She has expressive brown eyes and a perky little nose I just want to grab. (And sometimes break off and chuck to the floor before stomping on it.) Nevertheless, life without Lula is bland and colorless. I cannot get on without her. "You love me and you know it."

"Like I love a good scrub-down after radiation exposure," she replies.

"Like you love gangbang porn and fresh-baked chocolate chip cookies on a Friday night."

Little known fact: In high concentrations, chocolate is fatal for vampires. No different for dogs. In small doses, chocolate has a marijuana-type effect. Lula loves her chocolate chips as much as she does her kinky videos. I think it's a result of having been alive for so long. Our need to find new thrills can push our tastes a bit outside the norm. Personally, I seek adventure in spicy food. Sex and cookies lost their excitement when I was about a hundred years old.

"Lula?" Miriam appears behind me in the lobby.

"Mir!" The two women rush toward each other for a quick hug and start gabbing so fast I can hardly keep up. Except for the part where Miriam says...

"Did you hear?" Miriam bounces on her sensible black flats. "Michael and I are going to England to sort through his uncle's book collection!"

Lula doesn't miss a beat. "How exciting! I did *not* know." She gives me a side glance, her disapproving frown fast but furious.

Oops. Forgot to tell her. Or, perhaps, I didn't want to. Our mission is going to be focused on checking out the pits. Lula will not appreciate the extra responsibility and danger of bringing Miriam along.

"So are you coming to Michael's housewarming party tonight?" Lula asks.

"Oh…I'm not sure." Miriam crinkles her nose in distaste.

What the what, woman! "But you have to," I interject.

"I have so much to do," Miriam says apologetically, "and if I'm going to travel, that means packing. I'm meticulous when it comes to suitcase usage."

My testicles quiver, and I take a step back. How I love an organized suitcase, but I cannot allow her to skip out on our wedding night. There are charades to be had, cake to eat, sex to—*No. Stop. No sex.* This will be a ceremony and nothing more. *Down, mighty elm. Down, I say!*

"But Lula will be the only woman there, and I'm sure she doesn't want to be alone," I argue.

"Didn't you say your drama coach is coming?" Miriam asks.

"You're taking drama classes?" Lula laughs.

I narrow my eyes. "Yes. I mentioned it yesterday. Don't you remember? I said I invited a bunch of the guys from my troop."

Lula claps her hands together. "Fresh meat!" She turns to Miriam. "Then you should definitely *not* go. Less donkeys, more hay."

I shake my head. I know she can't be thrilled about my marriage, but this is a matter of life or death. I need my men guarding Miriam so I can take care of critical business. For example, right now there is a body in my car that needs a home. Then I must meet with Viviana and review her findings. After, Lula and I must go over our strategy for getting into the pits, and I still need to get the generals on a call.

"Miriam, Lula is just being greedy," I say. "You are still welcome, and I will take it as a personal insult if you do not attend this evening." I have everything worked out so that we can complete the ceremony before the men arrive. *It's a foolproof plan, just as long as my bride shows up.*

Lula laughs. "Mikey, why do you always sound like you have a stick up your ass? If Miriam doesn't want to go, then she doesn't."

Why the devil is she sabotaging me? The rage seeps into my veins.

"Oh no. Don't look so upset. Of course I'll be there." Miriam gives my arm a squeeze and it sends an erotic shiver down my spine, instantly cooling my rage, but heating up another zone. "I have some things to take care of for my new hires, but see you both tonight." Miriam heads to her office.

Lula and I watch her walk away and ensure she's out of earshot before whipping out our fangs.

"What the devil was that, Lula?"

"I was using a little reverse psychology so she'd agree to come. I can't believe that after everything, you still don't trust me," Lula hisses.

"How about a heads-up the next time you plan to help me out?" I hiss back.

"That would ruin the element of authenticity. So," she exhales, "why don't you shut your man hole and tell me what's first on the to-do list?"

"I need you to stay here and watch over Miriam while I—"

"Michael…" she whines in a hushed tone. "You brought me all the way to this sunny cesspool to babysit again?"

"I have no choice. We don't know where Alex and his army are or what they're planning."

"Since you're *king*, I'm now in charge of both Ohio and Arizona, Michael. Do you have any idea what's going on out there?" She points to the double glass door and lowers her voice again. "It's chaos. Everyone's in a panic, hoarding bagged blood, boarding up their windows, and getting ready to fight each other. No one trusts anyone, and it's up to the society leaders to keep the wheels on the vampire bus. I'm up to my eyeballs in emails and phone calls. And, unlike you, I don't have an assistant."

"Well…get one!"

"I'm too busy dealing with your shopping lists and babysitting your librarian."

"You *like* Miriam," I growl.

"So? I like a lot of people, but that's not going to keep the world from blowing up while you play charades and take your sweet time formulating a battle plan."

"I'm not going to battle, Lula." My words are just as much a shock to myself as they are to Lula, but now I realize why I've been so focused on getting out of being king.

She lifts two blonde brows. "Then who is?"

"We are getting the council members back. *They* will have to win this war."

Her mouth flaps for a moment. "Seriously?"

"What?"

"What if you can't get them back? What if they're dead already? Then what?" she snaps.

"They are alive. I know this because it would be foolish to dispose of such valuable assets. Also, Nice is still with us, so that indicates the leaders were not slaughtered."

"What if he's in on it, huh? A spy?"

"Nice? He's a pampered, spoiled loon. He doesn't want to go back to the old ways, because then there'd be no vampire romance novels or Netflix."

"Fine. You have a point, but in your scenario, you're proposing to free the other council members and have *them* fight the war. *Them* being vampires just like Nice."

"So?" What's her point?

"They are all crazy, Michael!" she whisper shouts. "They couldn't win a round of bingo even if the game was rigged."

"Oh, come now... I am certain they could manage cheating at bingo."

Lula slaps me across the cheek. "Wake up, you mental dump truck! You are our only hope to win this dance-off, so get that garbage out of your head. Forget the council leaders. Forget rescuing them. *You* know war. *You* know every devious trick in the book. Which is why the army and generals will follow you."

I groan with despair and rub the stinging flesh on my face. "I can't..."

"Why? Give me one good reason, Michael."

I look away, unwilling to speak the truth aloud. Not because I fear it, but because I know she will not understand. "Your faith in my abilities is misguided, Lula. We will move forward with my plan."

"You seriously want to leave our fate to a group of vampires who have the collective IQ of a box of Fruity Pebbles?"

They are ancient, much older than me. "They're more like a box of Grape-Nuts or maybe bran flakes."

"Fine!" She throws her hands in the air. "But you're making a big mistake."

"Perhaps you should trust I know what I'm doing." I clear my throat. "Now, if you don't mind, I have to dispose of Nice's dinner and then head to the office. I will be back around five to take over librarian duty."

Lula stomps away, likely to the beanbag kiddie area, where she'll pout for a while. "And don't forget to help Miriam with story time at three!" I yell, only to get hushed by a few of the moms milling about with their children.

"Sorry." I wave apologetically and head outside to my blue coffin containing one ripening body. Ironically, for the first time ever, I'm actually looking forward to a little alone time digging holes. I need to decompress and get my head straight. Too much is on the line for me to start making mistakes, and I'm beginning to realize that the Great War never truly ended for me. I am still living with the memories of the terrible things I did to make the world a better place. *I cannot repeat that chapter of my life. I simply cannot.*

But what if Lula is right? What if there is no other choice if we wish to win?

Hell. I hate being so good at killing.

                          ৡ ঙ

Just after two o'clock, I am covered in dirt and other things I prefer not to discuss, so I swing by my studio for a quick shower and change of clothes. I cannot believe how little I've accomplished today.

I open my narrow closet door and grab a light-blue button-down shirt and another pair of faded jeans. I slide them on and—

Wait. Where the hell is Nice? I open the closet again, hoping he's somehow hidden himself on a shelf up top or inside a shoe.

He's gone.

I plant my hand on my waist and shake my head. "Where the heck did he go?" I mutter. There are no signs of a struggle. No dust. Nothing but his lingering scent on my shirts.

I groan and spear my fingers through my wet hair. I don't have time for this. Luckily, Mr. Nice is a big boy; he can take care of himself.

I reach for the door handle and step into the hallway.

"Vandershorsthssssth!" Nice appears out of no-where, holding two overflowing shopping bags. "I found zi sexiest store ever!" He holds up the bag that says Bela Lugosi's Crypt.

"Wow. How...interesting."

"Not as interesting as the two-for-one sale on dickies." He rushes inside my studio—soon to be ex-studio—and I follow, closing the door behind me.

"Dickies, sir?"

He digs out a lace collar that isn't attached to a shirt. "You see? You can make it look like you have on a proper shirt underneath almost anything. I plan to wear *diss* with a black leather jumpsuit I found for your wedding." He slides out a shiny pleather leotard, not too dissimilar to the horrible outfit Lula has on today, except his has a terrifying S and M gimp vibe.

Thank God Nice thinks the ceremony is next week. By then, I'll either be dead or have come up with an excuse as to why my plans changed and I had to marry Miriam without him present.

Miriam... My heart accelerates. It's odd, but before I felt drawn to her. Now, being separated gnaws at me. *Must be the impending war. The danger has my senses heightened. Along with another body part.*

"So, *Beebeeiana* says the fun starts at seven?" Nice adds.

Viviana was here? And she told him about tonight? I feel a pit form in my stomach and plummet to my feet.

Nice narrows his eyes. "Yes. She stopped by to leave some munchies for you. She said she wasn't sure if you wanted blood in your new place until after the party—you might not want your bride to accidentally see it."

I can't believe Viviana spilled the wedding beans.

Nice continues, "So tell me, Vanderhorsthsssth, why would you lie to me about this wedding?"

Think quick. Think quick. "I meant no disrespect, Mr. Nice. But the truth is, I was not expecting you to show up last night, and given the dire situation, the ceremony I had planned is not at all worthy to be performed in front of you."

Nice's dark eyes hold fast to my face. Remember when I mentioned that vampires are terrible liars, but gifted lie detectors? Well, that goes quadruple for Nice. They say he can sniff out a lie from three states away.

Crap. Crap. Crap. I hope he buys my excuse. The only thing I have going for me is that I wasn't completely lying. Nice had hoped for a lavish, vampire fairytale wedding, the social event of the century. He'd even planned to rent horses and have them painted red to match his shirt and carriage. Some bean dip and a cooler filled with beer and single-serve wine with screw caps is hardly the romantic fantasy he's been pining for. But anything fancier, and Miriam might not buy my whole college-student-housewarming story.

"I'm very sorry, sir. Truly. But tonight is a formality so that I can ensure Miriam is treated like a queen and is afforded the protection of our army. In fact, she's so disappointed and heartbroken about not having her big Fanged wedding that she's pretending tonight is just a simple gathering at my new apartment. She's asked that we make it all seem like a game of charades."

"Ah! *Diss* is very smart. So, she will *habe* her real

wedding in a few months?"

"We hope. Because she won't consider us truly married until we have the real deal—vows, party, red horses."

"You know, Vanderhorsthsssth, I like your librarian more and more every day. You are very lucky." He sighs contentedly. "Are you sure you want her? Because I think I could—"

"She is mine," I snarl, before I can stop myself. It is dangerous to displease Nice, but when it comes to this, I simply do not care. He cannot have her. He shouldn't even joke about it.

Nice holds up his skinny pale hands. "*Oakzi dokzi.* In that case, I will be happy to play along at your non-wedding tonight."

"Thank you." I bow my head in gratitude. "There's just one more thing: Miriam is still sensitive about the whole vampire topic. So maybe just not mention it until she has had time to process."

Doubt flickers in Nice's soulless dark eyes. "You will perform the vampire marriage ceremony tonight, and your bride is pretending that you are not a vampire?"

"Well, when you put it like that, it sounds a bit odd. But, yes. Essentially."

"I like it! It's very weird. I will be there with *zi* bells on." He pulls out a string of tiny bells from his shopping bag.

"How very festive." I lift one brow.

"I must start getting ready now. Send *zi* car for me at seven. Yes?"

"I will send…" I have no one. No drivers, guards, nothing. "Uber."

"Tell Uber not to be late and to make sure there are snacks in the car. I always need a little something around seven."

There is no way I can make that happen. I can only hope that the driver isn't named Tim or Ted.

I don't have time to worry about this right now. I must get over to the office and start putting together the pieces of the puzzle: where our enemies are hiding, where they might attack, and any additional information about the council members' whereabouts.

"Mr. Nice, I wonder if you could answer a question."

"Yes?"

"How many others were with you?" I ask.

"All."

"All what?" I ask.

"All of the council members."

"From every region?" That's one hundred and forty-four—twelve regions, twelve council members each, with one chosen to sit on the international council.

"All in one big muddy hole. And you know how Gertrude the Gory is with her gas. She insists on eating vegetarians." He makes a sour face.

"They collected all the council members and

placed them in one spot, sparing only you. Why would they do that?" I am suspicious to say the least.

"It is a trap, you fool. They hope you will send your army to rescue everyone, and then attack."

That's precisely what I was thinking. Except... "So why did you not say so in the first place?"

"Didn't I?"

No. He did not. But what rouses my suspicion even more is the following:

1. How did the enemy know where to find all of the council members? They were in various locations—home, office, traveling, *Fanged Love* movie premier—yet Alex and his men rounded up each and every one.

2. The council members, as insane as they might be, are powerful. Fast. Strong. Cunning. How were they captured so easily?

3. Whoever is running the show seems to know a lot about the Great War and is using it to their advantage, i.e., rousing our kind's natural suspicion of each other to divide us, the pits, the fact that Clive was used to turbocharge their army.

Bottom line, our enemies know things only a person of great importance and power would know. Someone like...

I turn my head and stare at Nice. *No... He can't be their leader. He just can't.* As I said to Lula, he is simply too crazy, lazy, and spoiled to go back to the old days without credit cards and posh stores like Count Chocula's Shack of Fashion Doom or whatever.

It has to be someone else. Someone equally high-ranking. But who? Logic says it would have to be whoever wasn't taken prisoner.

"Are you certain, sir, that no one was missing? No one got away from this roundup?" I ask.

"No. I did a head count."

"But those pits are narrow and deep. I'm sure you were all standing on top of each other. Could you have missed someone during your head count?"

"No."

"So if I were to go there now, I'd find all one hundred and forty-three."

He shrugs. "No again. Half died to make more room. The Nice cannot be stepped on."

Jesus. "You killed half our leaders?"

He holds up a finger. "I merely suggested they kill themselves. It was either that or I was going to remove their limbs since no one confessed to stepping on my toe."

Hell, Nice has to be the one, then. He's the only option. *But why does my gut keep saying otherwise?*

"Thank you for understanding about the wedding." I step toward the door. "I will see you around seven, but feel free to come late."

"I wouldn't dream of it. I have missed the company of *your* librarian." He winks, and I do not like it one little bit.

Is that a dribble of drool coming down the side of his mouth? My jealousy goes through the roof. What game is he playing here?

"Thank you, sir. I cannot express my gratitude. Here you are, recovering from torture and being taken prisoner, yet you are still willing to support *my* very special relationship. With *my* wife to be."

Before I can blink, Nice is on me, his hands like iron claws around my neck. "My Fanged Love. Mine!" He snarls like a feral beast, his dark eyes bulging from his skull.

Instinctively, I raise my hands and remind myself there are two kinds of strength. One is of the body and the other of the mind. If I fight Nice, which I am willing to do for Miriam, I will likely lose, when all that matters is living another day. I cannot allow my kind to take over. For Miriam's sake.

"Are you…" I swallow hard, "all right, sir?"

"Miriam is mine." He shakes me so hard that my fangs clack against my lower teeth. What has possessed him?

"I think you are mistaken, Nice," I say in a firm, calm tone. "I am to wed her. Tonight. You yourself have been looking forward to our union, so how can she be yours?"

Nice blinks and shakes his head from side to side. "I…I…" He snaps his hand back, like I'm a venomous snake. "I don't know what came over me.

My biggest apologies, Vanderhorsthsssth."

I have no choice but to accept and leave before something else happens.

I dip my head and calmly go outside to my car. The pit in my stomach has turned into a tree stump. Mostly because I'm stumped. Why did he react like that?

I rest my head on the steering wheel. Something strange is going on. Or perhaps Nice was merely attempting to distract me from bigger issues…

—Army amassed.
—Council members taken from around the world and brought to one location.
—Obvious tactics being used from the Great War.
—Nice freed.

Could he, in fact, be a spy, sent to distract me?

I lift my head and push the engine's start button. I detest the lack of a manly engine sound.

"Wait. What if Nice is not the spy?" I mumble to myself and grip the steering wheel. "What if something else is going on?" Someone seems to be going out of their way to leave bread crumbs. Someone wants me to go to Blackpool with an army. *Or maybe stay away?*

Hell. I feel damned if I do react, damned if I do not.

My mind quickly shuffles through dozens of different facts, landing on one giant piece of the puzzle I have overlooked…

I am king.

I understand that our leaders are out of the game, but why me?

There's that one vampire…Glubdred or Gulberfield or…something that resembles the sound of making a loogie. He is third generation, fought in the war, and has led Eastern Europe for over three hundred years. He rejected a seat on his council because he felt more powerful ruling one territory than being one voice among twelve. A man like him, despite the unappealing name and physique of a lobster—unusually large hands and ruddy skin—is many times more qualified than myself for the role of king, no matter how legendary and virile I may be.

There is also Pussy. Her real name is Pousilda, but vampires can be like children. Once they pick up on something that amuses them, they do not let go so easily. *Such as childish nicknames.* Pousilda was the daughter of a wealthy Greek landowner. For all intents and purposes, she was a princess, and when her father was poisoned by a stable boy who loved Pousilda but wasn't good enough to wed her, she took over her father's place. She also killed the stable boy. Since that day, her ruthless hand has been legendary.

You want to get a man in line? Send Pussy.

Okay. Okay. That was a childish joke, unworthy of a man of my station, but I am merely repeating what is said about her.

I exhale and turn my attention back to the mysteries at hand: Me being chosen for king, Nice's role in all this, the enemy's real plans, and now…something I should have been questioning all along.

Miriam.

CHAPTER EIGHT

"Michael! Thank God you're here!" Viviana yanks me through the front door of our office building and slams the heavy steel door behind us. "You are not going to believe what I just found."

"Bad news. Incredibly bad, bad news," I respond drably. I'm quite certain this day is only going to get worse, and considering it is just past three in the afternoon, I should prepare for many more delights coming my way.

"Who told you?"

I shake my head. "A lucky guess."

"Everyone RSVPed to the ball."

I let that sink in. "Everyone?"

"Yes!" She nods frantically. "Do you know what that means?"

"Either we're barking up the wrong tree or—"

"They knew we'd check! Whoever is behind this is in our heads." She taps the side of her skull.

Feeling dumbfounded, I walk over to her desk in the middle of the room and sit. "Fuck."

"Michael!" She gasps. "Such language is not becoming of a king."

"Who the hell cares, woman?" I grumble.

"Oh, now you're in trouble." She folds her arms over her chest. "I might be a vampire, but I'm still a lady who doesn't approve of potty mouths."

"Sorry," I mutter miserably. "You're right."

"Apology accepted. Now. What are we going to do?"

I feel like they are anticipating my moves and throwing out red herring after red herring. "Have you swept our office for bugs?"

"Yes. Of course."

"How about our phones? Could they be tapped?" I wonder aloud.

"Not likely, considering how often we change them, but you know how careful we all are about discussing sensitive business."

I groan. I taught Alex everything I know, but this feels different. Vampires can be very intuitive. Some come equipped with centuries of experience, which allows them to easily predict the outcome of a situation. But we are *not* mind readers. Once again, something simply doesn't feel right about this situation.

What the devil is going on? The answer is probably staring me right in the face.

I take a deep breath. All right, everything so far has had one thing in common: It's kept me guessing. And it has also prevented me from taking any real action because I am unsure of what to do. I have no one to fight because we do not know where our enemies are. I cannot rescue the council members if they're simply being used as bait. I haven't rallied the generals because I am reluctant to truly take over and fight another war, perhaps the reason I was chosen as king in the first place. Again, it is as if someone already knew how I would react.

So, given all this, my only choice is to take action that would be…uncharacteristic. And make sure I keep as much of my plans to myself as I can.

"We're going to have to assume that everyone is a spy," I say. "We will no longer speak of plans."

"Then how will we coordinate anything?"

"Kings do not coordinate. They give orders. Which you will follow without question, as will everyone else." I lift my chin. "Spread the word. We are in a state of emergency and our vampocracy is over. We are officially in a dicvampireship."

"That just sounds like a dick is in charge."

"Exactly. And what were you just saying about language?"

"Sorry." She glances down at her shoes.

"Please, just get the word out: Heads will dust if my orders aren't obeyed." If I can keep everyone guessing, I just might be able to outsmart the other side. Let them see a piece of the puzzle, but keep the big picture to myself.

"Yes, sir!" she says cheerfully.

I grab a piece of paper from her printer to jot down a bunch of instructions—buy plane tickets to Blackpool, care and feeding instructions for Mr. Nice, and snacks for tonight's wedding. I hand the list over. "Got it covered?"

She nods.

"Good. Now burn that and don't be late." This vampire is done being playdough. I am molding the terrain and taking control of this farce.

Darn it! Lula was right again. Maybe I am the only option we have to win this. But why does she always have to be righter than me?

I spend the rest of the afternoon talking to the generals and explaining that we are going to have to change the way things are done if we have any hope of formulating a successful defense. Encrypted orders will be sent to each general. I will be the only one with a full view of the game plan. This way, if I suspect one general is not on our side, I can misdirect him. But under no circumstances will anyone know the entirety of my plans. With any luck, this will also flush out the spies. If a piece of information is acted upon, I will know who is the mole.

My first order of business is sending a message to Otto, our general in Europe, that I will be arriving in two days' time to discuss strategies. I do not mention the pits or Nice being here in Phoenix.

Viviana has purchased plane tickets, but they are merely to cover my true plans. I have called in a favor from an old friend and quietly arranged my own transportation. The benefit to being a vampire as old as myself is that I have several secret identities, which enable me to travel under a different name. After the party, I will take Miriam, Lula, and four guards with me to "a night club." I will take their phones, and we will get on a chartered plane to Liverpool. Upon arrival, I will leave Miriam on the plane with the guards, and Lula and I will scope out the location of the council members. If any are in fact still there, then I will summon Otto to a location nearby and ask that he bring a few hundred men. We will free the remaining council members, divide them into groups, and send them to secure locations only myself and Lula will know. From there, I can help them set up remote offices and get them back in control of their regions. Once everything is in place, I will return to Arizona and flip the power back to them so I may focus on my own priorities: keeping those I care about safe. *And…figuring out why Miriam is not only a danger magnet, but a vampire magnet, too.*

"Michael?" Viviana sticks her head into my office. "I need to take care of a few errands, so if you don't mind, I'll be taking off early." She hands me a pink Post-it that reads, *See you at your new apartment. Going to get everything set up.*

I nod. "See you tomorrow."

I finish up writing the last of the instructions for each of my generals. The emails are locked with passwords only they will know: the dates they were turned. I can only hope that our enemies do not have access to such information. The only reason I have it is because the prior leader of the Arizona Society of Sunshine Love was a kiss-ass. He had Viviana research the dates and sent them all little Happy Vampiversary gift baskets each year.

I send the messages off, shut down for the day, and head over to the library. By the time I arrive, Miriam and Lula are just coming out the front door and locking up. From the looks of their smiles and laughter, they had a good time today.

Good. Our wedding day should be a happy one, even if my bride does not know what we are about to do.

I contentedly watch the two women giggling away, and then something happens. Miriam flips her long hair over her shoulder, and it's in slow motion. The sun bounces off the golden hues of her silky blonde strands. She smiles, and it radiates from within, igniting a warmth deep inside my chest. Her soulful eyes twinkle with a keen awareness.

So lovely. I've noticed there's an intelligence in those eyes she tries to mask. Perhaps that is what lures me in. Her secrets make me feel like she is the mystery I was born to unlock.

I stand there frozen, completely captivated. Breathless. Wondering how in the hell I am ever going to let her go, but knowing I must. Tonight we marry, and if I want to keep my sanity, I cannot let my heart wish for more than that. A ceremony. Not that she wants a real marriage, but if she did, it would not work. I am a vampire and she needs to stay human. Those two things do not mix.

"Hey, Mikey!" Lula says. "I gotta run, but see ya later at the shindig."

"Where are you off to?" Miriam asks Lula, shoving her keys into her little brown purse.

"I have a few errands to run, but I'll be right behind you." Lula gives Miriam a hug and walks off in the direction of downtown.

"So." I stand there on the sidewalk, a few feet away from the woman I am about to wed in a matter of hours, while cars zoom by on the busy street. *My hands are shaking. Why are my hands shaking? None of this is real. You'd best remember that, man.*

"What are you doing here?" she asks.

I shove my hands in my jeans pockets, forcing myself to deny any and all urges to give tonight any further indecent or unrealistic thoughts.

"Oh. Uh…well," I reply, "I brought you to work this morning. Seemed only befitting that I take you home."

"Don't you have a party to prepare for?" she asks.

"It's more of a small gathering. It's all taken care of."

"Still, I'm sure you need to heat up food, put out plates and stuff. I'll just grab an Uber." Miriam hitches her purse strap higher on her shoulder and starts digging out her phone.

Over my cold undead body. "Wouldn't dream of it. I'll take you home to change, and you can come with me to my place."

"Then I'll just have to take an Uber home tonight, and it's going to be late."

This is what I love—I mean *enjoy*—about Miriam. She is smart and hard to fool. It also irritates the hell out of me when I need to fool her. "Very well. You caught me."

She narrows her big brown eyes in suspicion.

I continue, "I was going to surprise you later, but considering your love of packing...we're leaving tonight!"

"For the UK?" Her eyes grow even bigger.

"Yep. A friend owes me a favor and offered his jet."

"Your friends have private planes?" she questions. "And what did you do to deserve that kind of favor?"

I helped him win the US Civil War. "It's a long story, but we're old, *old* friends." I swipe my hand dismissively through the air. "And hey, considering how tight money is for you and me, I thought this would be the perfect compromise. Free flight. We look at the book collection. We're back before we even have jet lag." *What a load of improbable crap. I hope she buys it.*

"What about the library? I haven't had a chance to train the new people or anything. They're supposed to come in tomorrow."

"Call and tell them to come when you return," I suggest. "You'll only be gone a day. Two tops. I'm sure everyone knows how to return books through that little slot."

"I don't know, Michael." She fidgets with the strap of her purse. "I've had the library closed a lot because of all that land developer garbage. Then there was your cult, and—"

"I understand. Completely. Why don't you stay here, then?" I hope this reverse psychology trick works for me like it did for Lula earlier. "I can text you photos of any books I think might be worth something. Besides, I'm sure all those first edition Jane Austens he bragged about were counterfeit."

"Jane Austens?" Her voice perks up.

"My uncle was a fan of the classics, but I bet there are a ton of those autographed *Pride and Prejudices* around." I have no idea if this is true. I only know that Miriam needs to stay by my side as much as possible. *Or…maybe it is I who needs to be by her side.* After Nice's oddball behavior earlier, I'm feeling less and less sure about having anyone guard her. For certain, I do not want to be halfway around the world while she remains here, so far from reach. At least if she comes with me, we will only be separated for a few short hours, and we will be in the same geographical area.

"You know what? You're right. I can make this work," she says.

The non-pushy technique was successful? "So

you're coming?"

"I hardly take vacations, even during the holidays. I'm sure my patrons will understand."

I try not to appear too excited. "Great. Then let's get to your place so you can pack a few things, and we'll head to my new apartment."

We go to my little blue car and, screw me, but I feel something shifting between me and Miriam. I cannot quite put my finger on it, but I am on edge during the entire drive to her house about twenty minutes away.

The feeling only grows as I wait in her living room while she packs. It is almost like these thoughts of "us" is creating a reaction. Is it inside me? Inside her? Both?

"Okay. All ready!" Miriam comes out of her bedroom carrying a backpack, dressed in tight jeans and a white, slightly see-through blouse with a lacy white brassiere underneath. I almost lose my mind.

Sweet devil of lust, what is she wearing? She looks sexier than hell in jeans—the curve of her hips and shape of her body—and the view of her brassiere, albeit obscured, only makes me think about what lies underneath. *Boobies.*

I release a deep sigh of appreciation. I so very much love boobies. And hers look like two ripe pieces of fruit at the market, just begging to be squeezed.

God, I cannot believe I am to marry this woman, but cannot touch her. And by touch, I mean bed her. *She is too damned beautiful.*

"So, do I look all right?" she asks, a glint of flirtation in her eyes and a wicked little smile on her plump lips.

Regrettably, I am an open book, and she's just read my pages. She knows I like what I see. I cannot pretend otherwise. *Perhaps the drool running down the side of my mouth was a giveaway.*

But why is she doing this to me? Why the sudden change in her behavior?

I know nothing about the connection between us, but I do know it's there. This is proof. It has to be. Because, for the first time since we've met, I'm pulling away. I cannot allow myself to forget the truth: She can never be my wife—not for real. To do so would destroy her and, frankly, me. *To marry a human, only to watch her die after a few short decades?* Sounds like the sort of tragedy a man should avoid at all costs. Nevertheless, it is almost as if she senses my internal struggle. I am trying to put an emotional barrier between us, and she's whipping out the carrots. *So many carrots*, I groan internally.

For certain, this is a new dynamic between us. Mouse chasing cat. Regardless of the reason, I cannot give in.

But she looks so...so damned tasty. I want a nibble. Just one.

"Su-sure," I stutter. "You look, yanno, okay."

"You look flushed. Are you sweating?"

Vampires do not sweat. We can, but we generally do not—one of the perks of being cold-blooded. "I, uh…ate some really spicy peppers for lunch today."

"You really need to lay off the hot food, Michael. You probably have a hole in your stomach."

I should be so lucky. It would provide me with a distraction. "You ready?" I jerk my head toward the front door.

"Sure!" She actually sounds excited. "Got my passport, laptop for looking up information on the books, and some good reading for the flight."

I take her backpack. "Oh, that reminds me. I wanted to keep the charter plane a surprise for Lula. So if you'd keep that to yourself?" Really, I do not want to discuss any plans in public. I am unsure of who might be listening.

"Lula's coming? How wonderful."

"Indeed," I reply, ignoring all thoughts of wanting to be alone on my wedding night with my bride.

"I have to say, Michael, she is one special woman to stay friends with you after your messy breakup."

Messy breakup? Lula and I were never in a relationship. All that had been a lie because I needed to explain why Lula hung around so much. There were other reasons for the lie, too, but it all came back to bite me in the ass. I truly wish I could stop lying to Miriam. I know she is unwilling to hear the truth, but my life would be much easier if I did not have to make up stories to cover my activities.

"What did she tell you?" I refrain from growling.

"Nothing," she says innocently. "Just that it's over for good between you two."

Did Miriam ask Lula if I am single? "How did this subject come up?"

Miriam offers a shrug. "Can't really remember."

She's lying. She did ask. Once again, I find myself having to tamp down any thoughts of taking this further. Whatever the hell *this* is.

"Are you ready?" I ask, wanting to change subjects.

"You have no idea." Miriam sets the security alarm and trots outside. I have never seen such a spring in her step, and for a moment, I am happy, too. Until I remember that it is all a ruse—the party, the trip, everything Miriam knows about me.

I do not know when. I do not know how. But if I cannot have Miriam, at the very least, I want to have an honest relationship with her. This bullcrap needs to end.

Of course, there's a strong possibility that if she ever learned the truth about tonight, she might not forgive me. *Duped into marrying a vampire. Sounds like the title of another Fanged Love book.*

CHAPTER NINE

"Shouldn't we wait until your other friends arrive before we play?" Miriam says, from the lackluster-beige couch in my new living room.

I hand her a glass of red wine, a necessary prop for the ceremony. I ignore the fact she's batted her eyelashes at me at least five times since we arrived and that this time makes six.

"No. They won't mind," I reply. "Plus, I could really use a warm-up. I haven't played this game in a very long time."

Viviana and Lula are chatting it up in the kitchen, which is part of the main room, divided into three sections—dining area, living room, and, of course, the kitchen. The furnishings are nice and new, but basic. Lots of grays and khaki with a light hardwood floor. The new stainless steel appliances are missing the roaches I have become accustomed to, which is a big plus. A few vibrant desertscapes liven up the place, and a flat-screen TV mounted to the wall is on mute but set to the Weather Channel.

Wonderful. A storm is rolling in. I pray it will not impact our departure. Just as I pray that whatever's happening between Miriam and me won't throw me off. I must stay focused on tonight's task: Marry. Get guards. Head to plane, already on standby at airport.

"Lula, Viviana," I call to get their attention, "you two are in need of a little charades warm-up, right?"

Both women give me the deer-in-headlights look.

Yes, ladies, it is nuptial showtime. Chop-chop, I think to myself.

"Errr…yeah. I would love to play," says Lula.

"Me too," Viviana chimes in. "You know us drama coaches, always looking for any excuse to show off our acting skills. Should I do some Shakespeare for you?"

With Miriam's head turned, I mouth, "*Cool it!*" to Viviana. She's laying it on a little thick. *This pre-party couldn't get any more stressful or weirder if—*

The front door flies open. "Vanderhorstsssth! I am here!"

Oh dear Jesus. It is Nice, and he is an hour early. I arranged a driver to pick him up at seven, so what the heck is he doing here?

And what the hell is he wearing? It is the black pleather gimp suit with a lace dickie. *And a regular dickie, too.* The crotch of his pants is so tight we can see everything. Two golf balls and a flashlight.

Well, at least he's got that going for him. Because the clothes? Not so attractive.

"Come in, sir, make yourself comfortable." I

rush to close the door behind him and whisper, "We are about to perform the ceremony. Just remember, she wants to pretend that it's nothing more than a game."

"Your ruse is safe with me." Nice locks his lips and throws away the key. His eyes then lock onto Miriam, and he zips over. "My sweet, sweet librarian." He takes her hand and kisses the top. "You are even more beautiful than I remember."

"Uh...thank you?" She tugs her hand away. "Mr. Nice, was it?"

"Yesss... You remember me," he hisses in a low voice. "Just as I remember you. You and your sexy collection of books." His dark eyes flicker with lust.

Is he hitting on her? "Can I get you something to drink, sir?" I sneer.

"No." He continues beaming down with his beady, sharklike eyes at Miriam, who is silently panicking—flushed cheeks and the smell of fear wafting from her skin. She's only met Nice once, but it was enough to terrify her and make an impression.

"So nice to see you again." Her back stiffens.

"Yes...so *Nice*. But perhaps we should ensure there are many more encounters. Would you like that?" The corners of his mouth twitch with a wicked smile, and it dawns on me that maybe he is not here to witness the ceremony.

He's here to steal the bride. My already cold blood turns to ice. "Lula, why don't you give Mr.

Nice a tour of the apartment." There are only three rooms—this one, the bathroom, and the bedroom, but it will buy me a few seconds to think. I have to do something.

"I have all I wish to see right here." Nice continues salivating over Miriam like she's a warm, freshly baked chocolate chip cookie. Meanwhile, Miriam looks like a tiny animal with its leg caught in a trap, not knowing what to do.

I cannot believe this. If Nice is a spy, here to sabotage me, then he is a genius and has already won. If he's merely here to steal my woman—I mean, *my librarian*—I am still on the losing side. I cannot make a move against him without Miriam seeing. Also, the odds of beating him in a hand-to-hand situation are not good. Not zero percent either, but not good. He is much, much older than me. Yes, I am second generation, but Nice is faster and lived in the days when men killed each other with their bare hands. None of this…guns and swords crap. They used rocks and threw clay pots. Or so I hear. *Really must catch up on the Byzantine era.*

"Mr. Nice, sir, if I may have a word with you in the other room?"

He waves me off. "No, *sank* you." He takes a seat beside Miriam and scoots so close that he's nearly on top of her.

My jealousy turns into an angry bull, kicking up dirt and ready to charge.

Miriam scoots all the way over to the armrest, but he nudges over, closing the gap.

"So, have you read zi latest Fanged Love, *Fangless in Seattle?*" Nice asks.

"Oh, uh…I'm almost done," Miriam responds in a shaky voice.

"And what did you think?" He raises a dark brow.

"Well," she swallows anxiously, "I was a little surprised that the author put out a third book so fast. I mean, it usually takes her a year for each edition."

"Yes…" Nice's dark eyes twinkle with sadistic delight. "Toothpicks glued to the eyelids can have that effect on a writer."

Is that what he did to that poor Mimi Jean woman? I only hope she is somewhere safe now. *Unlike Miriam.*

Sonofabitch, I must do something. And the only thing I can think of is to start the ceremony now. Not to marry her, but to create a distraction.

"Well!" I clap my hands together. "Now that we have Mr. Nice here, it's the perfect opportunity to begin charades."

"I will be on her team." Nice puts his arm around Miriam, and I wonder how she's managed to not wet herself. I also wonder how I've refrained from jumping Nice. *Take your filthy dead hands off her, Nice.*

"Actually, sir," I say, "this is merely a warm-up.

No teams. And I'll go first."

I wave Lula and Viviana over to the loveseat perpendicular to the sofa, which is holding a frightened Miriam and a horny-as-hell Nice.

Lula and Viviana both give me shifty-eyed looks—the sort one uses when they want to ask what the heck is going on but can't. My response is to remain calm.

And here I was, worried about pulling off the ceremony with Miriam. This is much worse. Nice has come to stake a claim on my librarian.

"Well, do not keep us waiting, Vanderhorsthssth." Grinning like a mad loon, Nice squeezes his arm tighter around Miriam. Her eyes go wide like two Frisbees.

If those Frisbees were saying "Help. Meee…"

The tension in the room spikes to defcon 4. Except for Nice, who seems lost in his own happy little bubble.

"Yes. One moment," I say. "I am coming up with a good one for you. Got it." I start miming an old-fashioned movie camera.

"Movie!" Lula barks out.

I nod and hold up four fingers and then repeat.

"Four words. Fourth word." Viviana slides to the edge of the sofa. Her body language reminds me of a spring-loaded mousetrap.

I look directly at Lula. This is the part where I would like to say we know each other so well that she can read my mind, but the truth is I am about to take a huge risk. I can only hope she sees, as I do, that there is only one move to be had, and we both must do our parts.

You keep Viviana safe, Lula. Protect her, runs through my thoughts.

I continue with the charade. I take my hands and wave them sideways through the air, wiggling my fingers.

"You are a magician?" Nice says gleefully, enjoying the game.

I shake my head no and then glance at Lula. I blow hard, continuing the movements with my hand.

"Wind! *Choo* are the wind!" Nice barks out.

I nod yes and lock eyes with Lula once more. She gives me a look of horror as if to say, *Don't do it. Don't do it...*

Sadly, I must. I hold up one finger.

"First word," says Viviana.

I pause, rallying my composure. *Do it, man. Just freaking do it.* I exhale and make like my fingers are walking on the palm of my other hand.

"A Stroll in the Garden of Windpipes!" Nice yells out. "A Walk on the Windy Glacier of Death! Dances on Piles of Breezy Flesh."

Those are all movies? What sort of crap is this man into? *Wait. Never mind. Don't want to know.*

"Darn. None of those are four words." Nice scratches the smooth pale skin of his cheek. "Hold on. I've got it! *Gone with the Wind*!"

"Yep." I swoop down and grab Miriam, throwing her over my shoulder. As fast as I can move, which is literally as fast as the wind, I am out the front door and bolting for the nearest exit leading down to the parking garage below the building. Miriam is screaming bloody murder, and I am unsure if it is because we are moving so fast or because I've just gone caveman on her. Either way, all that matters is saving her life. Nice has lost his marbles, and I cannot think of anything more dangerous than him wanting to make her his Fanged Love.

We arrive to my car, and I quickly toss her in the trunk. "Sorry about the smell!"

In a split second, I am in the driver's seat and starting the engine. The electric car hums to life. I back out, throw the car into drive, and hit the accelerator. All the while, Miriam is yelling in the trunk and my cell phone is ringing. I screech out of the garage, onto the street, and take a hard right in the direction of the private airport.

The call is from Lula.

I hit the button on my console, and her voice pours over the speakers. "Whatthehell, Michael!"

"Lula! Are you and Viviana all right?"

"Yes, but Jesus! Give me a heads-up next time."

"I did. *Gone with the Wind.*"

"I thought you were going to pounce on Nice, not run away, you idiot!"

"How could you think that? He's too dangerous. I couldn't risk fighting him with Miriam right there."

"Well, I hope you're driving the speed of light because Nice took off after you, howling for his librarian. What the hell's gotten into him?"

"I wish I knew. Because this is the last thing I need to deal with." Perhaps they did something to Nice when he was taken prisoner. Or maybe he has been putting on an act the entire time and this is all meant to distract me. It seems to be the enemy's MO.

"Well, I don't think it matters what you want because he's coming for you," Viviana says in the background.

I hit the freeway entrance and push the tiny car as fast as it can go. I am certain Nice can outrun this flea with wheels, but he doesn't know which direction I went, nor does he know his way around town.

At least, I hope not.

"Get out of my apartment," I command, "and get to the office. Stay there until I contact you." Interesting fact: Every society's headquarters is built for two purposes. One, to conduct business, and two, to act as a fortress. The brick walls are five feet thick and reinforced with solid steel beams every six inches around the inside perimeter. The heavy steel front door has hinges a tank could not bust through, and the roof is constructed from more steel beams. There is a good reason there are no windows, and this is one of them. They will be safe there until I figure out what to do.

"Michael! Whatthehell! Let me out!" Miriam yells.

"I'll call you later, Lula." I hang up, wincing. This is not the way I wanted the evening to go. I glance in my rearview mirror and continue violating every traffic law possible in my little buggy.

"Michael! I am revoking your library card! You are dead to me!" Miriam yells.

"I'm already dead," I mutter to myself. And if I am lucky, she will not be joining me.

Fifteen minutes later, I am pulling into the gated driveway at the private airstrip. I stop at the guard station, flip on the radio, and set it to some rock station. I crank it up to full blast before lowering the window to greet the guard.

"Well, hello there!" I yell. "I'm Miguel Vontrape. I have a reservation!" Miguel is one of my many secret identities. I used this particular one quite often when I worked for Clive in my detective days.

The older guy in the brown uniform looks at me like I'm mad, but I assume I am not the first obnoxious person to pull into this airfield with millions of dollars of private jets.

I hand him my fake passport for inspection, and he hands it back. "Have a nice flight, Mr. Vontrape. Your plane is waiting over there." He points to a large white executive jet with the interior lit up. A welcoming orange light pours through the open door above the staircase.

"Thanks!" I roll up the window and lower the volume on the music. Miriam is quiet now, but I do not believe for one second it is because she is through yelling at me. I am also certain that Nice has not given up either. If we're lucky, *very* lucky, we will escape.

I pull up beside the stairs and spot the pilot in the cockpit.

Thank goodness. I grab Miriam's backpack, the one she left on the floor of my car, and hit the trunk release. I do not bother with taking my car keys because there is no time to park the Cookie Monster, and I'm certain the staff will need to move it.

I dash outside just as Miriam is kicking open the hatch. Her dirty blonde hair is a mess, and her face is blistering with fury.

"Come on." I grab her wrist and yank her out of the trunk so fast that I nearly knock the wind from her. "Sorry."

"Michael! Let me go." She somehow manages to dig her heels into the asphalt, and I'm forced to release her so I do not snap off her sweet little arm.

I move to grab her again, but she stumbles back. "Stop! What are you doing!"

Crap. I cannot afford for her to make a scene. The airport might alert the authorities. The pilot is an acquaintance, so I am not too worried about him.

I grab her firmly by the shoulders. "You must trust me. We only have a few seconds before Nice finds us."

Miriam's eyes are wide with fear, but her mouth and body language are rife with anger. "What the hell is going on? And…" she jerks her body back, "get your hands off me."

"We do not have time for this." I hear a gust of air one block away. It could be just that, or it could be *him*. "Goddammit, Miriam!" I scold. "I am a vampire. Nice is a vampire. And he is much, much older than me, so if we do not get on that goddamned plane, he will take you as his bride, and there won't be a damned thing I can do about it!"

Miriam blinks up at me, and I can see the wheels turning in her head. She can't quite believe what I'm saying, but how else can she explain the way I moved her from my apartment to my car in two seconds flat?

"Holy Christ. You really are a vampire," she mutters under her breath.

"Yes! And I do not want to lose you. Can we go now?" I flash a nervous glance over my shoulder. "Because I assure you this is not the time nor the place to get into details unless you want to become bride of the gimp and spend your days reenacting scenes from the *Fanged Love* wedding."

"Oh God. No."

"Excellent response." I scoop her up and dash up the staircase, tossing her into the first row of seats before shutting the door. "Go! Fly! Get us into the air, Fernando."

Fernando is an old friend, originally from what is now known as the Dominican Republic. He was taken as a young boy by slave owners in the 1800s and then one day came across a vampire, now dusted, who believed in the old ways. For some reason, he liked Fernando and turned him rather than kill him. It didn't take long for Fernando to end his maker, who enjoyed snacking on anyone he pleased, including other slaves. Fernando would then go on to help win the US Civil War—behind the scenes—and free the slaves. Since then, he has been a lawyer, a doctor, and a few other professions. Now he owns one of the world's largest fleets of private jets and enjoys flying them any chance he gets. He is one of the few men I trust in this world, but even so, I have not told him a thing, and Fernando is too smart to ask. The less he knows, the better.

"I'll get us in the air as quickly as I can." Fernando ducks into the cockpit and gets to work.

I hear Miriam in the background, shuffling through her backpack, but my focus is on the gate and the road leading into the airfield. Nice could stop this plane with a flick of a finger—remove a tire, crack a window, pull off the engine.

"Come on. Come on…" My heart races as we begin to advance.

Oh no.

A white streak moves outside, punches through the chain-link fence, and comes straight for us.

"Go!" I yell. "Go!" But the plane is merely inching along, making a slow turn toward the runway.

"Vanderhorsthssssth!" Nice stops right below the window and points up at me. "Give her back! She is my Fanged Love. You are not good enough for her and her books!"

Don't I know it. "You'll have to kill me first, Nice." Despite the noise of the engines, I can hear him just fine, and I know he can hear me.

He moves alongside the plane, keeping his eyes locked on me. "Easy. I am much older than you. And a much better dresser."

He really thinks that? Or that it matters? "But I am the son of Cluentius Boethius. I am over four hundred years old and have slaughtered thousands on the battlefield, so if you think I'm going to hand over the woman I love without a fight or that I fear you and your shiny pants, think again."

Wait. Did I just declare my love for her? More importantly, did I mean it? Obviously I did, because I said it.

Nice balls his fist, and I prepare to knock out the door. If we fight, it will be outside. Not in here where Miriam will be harmed.

"Jesus, go away. Just go away!" Miriam yells.

I glance over my shoulder and notice Miriam peering out the last window at the far end of the cabin.

Nice sees her, and it is as if he's hit by a brick in the face. He drops his arm and stares at her, mesmerized. I do not know what they did to Nice or why Miriam has become his latest fixation, but it is clear he has lost his faculties.

The plane completes the turn, lining up with the runway, and Fernando punches it. Nice disappears from view, and I can only hope he hasn't decided to grab a wheel and go for a ride.

We'll know in a moment. I still my body, listening for any sounds. The plane roars off the ground and into the air. I hear the gears and flaps move.

"Is everything okay?" I call out.

"Yes," Fernando replies.

"Good. Keep going."

"Same destination, my king?"

East. "For now."

I close the cockpit door and turn. At the rear of the tilted plane, Miriam is standing with her back to the wall, her face lacking any sign of emotion.

"You're really a vampire?" she whispers. I can hear her just fine, though a human would not.

I nod.

"And Jeremy?" she asks.

I nod again.

"And Lula, Viviana, Nice—all vampires?"

Another nod. This time I take a step closer, but she stiffens.

I hold my hands up. "I would never hurt you." And I would give anything to hear her thoughts. At the moment, I cannot even sense her emotions. I am much too charged up with my own.

Cautiously, I approach, doing my best not to allow the stern, protective, angry vampire in me to show through, but adrenaline is coursing in my veins, demanding I take action even if the threat is gone. Whatever that was back there with Nice has just cost me dearly. I cannot leave Miriam under the protection of my army because we did not marry. I cannot run off and play detective, leaving Miriam alone. No matter where we go, there will be vampires, and I do not know which ones are against us. She will have to remain by my side from here on out.

I stop a few feet in front of her and stare down, waiting patiently for her to say something.

"You're really four hundred years old?" she finally asks, blinking rapidly. The tone in her voice is quiet, restrained.

"Give or take a few years," I reply in a low, calm voice.

"And you just saved me from becoming that insane goth man's plaything."

"Yes." I nod, overtaken with the urge to hold her, simply to assure myself she truly is standing here with me unharmed. I would have died fighting Nice, and I would have done so gladly; however, that would have only left Miriam for his taking if I'd lost.

"You said you love me." It's not a question, but

I know she's questioning it.

"I believe I did." I suddenly pick up on her emotions again. I can feel she wants me. She is afraid to, but like me, she can't hide it any longer.

"And this—this thing between us, is it normal?" she asks.

I shake my head, because I honestly do not know.

"But you feel it, too, don't you?" she asks.

"I do."

Her shoulders fall. "Thank God. I thought I was losing my mind. I can't stop thinking about you."

I am too caught up in the moment to care, but it strikes me as odd that she is so unfazed by my confession. I am a vampire, and she doesn't seem to care. Perhaps because like me, she's too overwhelmed by thoughts of another sort.

The scent of her arousal fills my nostrils and it is more than I can take. I slide my hand to the back of her neck and close the gap between us. "You have no idea how long I have wanted to do this." I cover her mouth with mine, and the warmth of her body instantly ignites a hundred different sensations—adrenaline, lust, fear, need, and so many other things I do not have time to think about. My entire body explodes with libidinous sensations.

My tongue slides past her lips, and she stills for a fraction of a second, perhaps shocked by the coolness of my mouth, which only lasts a moment while her heat transfers into me. Then, she kisses me back, squeezing my biceps with her small hands.

That's right, I think to myself, *touch me*. Because I intend to reciprocate fully. I have waited far too long for this.

I reach for her gauzy white blouse and work the buttons loose, quickly shedding the garment to the floor. She reaches for my blue button-down and does the same. Perfectly in tune to each other, we pause our kiss to take each other in before we are back to the ravenous, hungry pace.

I run my hand up the side of her waist and savor the delicate soft skin under my fingertips before making a small tear in the front of her brassiere. I have no patience for clasps tonight.

I cup her warm breast and enjoy the weight and feel in my hands. Her skin is silky and hot, and I want to bury myself in her. I want to lose myself in her sweet scent and the sound of her beating heart.

I help her undo the button of my jeans and shed my pants before picking her up. I have imagined being with her so many times, I can hardly believe this is happening.

She wraps her legs around my waist and presses her pillowy soft breasts against my hard chest. I want to tear away her jeans, but if I do, I'll be inside her before we're even lying down. Yes, in this moment, I am thinking of my own selfish pleasure, of relieving the ache of my lust, but I am no fool, and I am certainly no twenty-year-old lad. I learned long ago that the sweetest release takes work, it takes time, but it happens when you are sheathed deep inside a woman while she climaxes. There is nothing better.

I push the button on one of the seats toward the back, extending it to the inclined position. I lower her onto the soft white leather and break away from our kiss long enough to peel away her jeans and undergarment. She looks up at me with those deep brown eyes, her long hair loose around her shoulders, and I lose my mind. I do not recall ever seeing a more beautiful woman so wild with desire.

She stares, drinking in my nude form, including my manhood. I know I must seem like a beast in this moment. Every muscle in my body is pulsing with tension and need.

"Wow. You are really hot, Michael."

I glance down at my six-pack. It pales in comparison to her curves and feminine beauty, but I do not say a word. I am not in a talking mood.

I lay myself over her, settling between her thighs, and return to our voracious kisses. With a prod of her hips, she presses her most intimate spot against the base of my throbbing shaft. It sends me off a cliff.

I take her hands, press them over her head, and kiss my way down her neck, settling my lips over the rapid pulse just beneath her delicate skin.

She stills, suddenly realizing what I am about to do. I would explain it to her, I would tell her it is perfectly safe, and she will enjoy it, but this is the sort of thing one must experience firsthand.

I thrust myself inside her and bite down. She gasps, and I feel her tense beneath me. She tastes sweet. *But not so innocent.* Though the lack of spicy heat on my tongue confirms what I've always known; she is special and purehearted. For a devilish prick like me, she is a sinful treat I will never tire of.

It only takes a moment for my sweet librarian to let go and give in to the pleasure—the suction of my mouth coupled with my movements deep inside her. Some call it a trick of the trade, I call it a perk of lying with a man like myself.

I thrust with more forceful strokes, completely lost in the ecstasy of plunging into such delicious silky warmth, while our two bodies writhe in an animalistic rhythm.

The air fills with her moans and my deep grunts. She digs the heels of her feet into the backs of my thighs, urging me to go harder, deeper. I must be careful not to go too far. She is not like me. She is fragile and alive. So alive.

I give her what she wants and take what she gives, one erotic pounding at a time. I can't get enough of her, of the friction of her around me.

Suddenly, I feel her body tensing. I break the seal on her neck and press my forehead to hers, careful not to let our lips touch. She will not taste what I taste. It will only remind her of who's inside her. A vampire. A man who should not be alive but is and has killed again and again to stay that way.

But hell, I want her. I want this. And I've never wanted anything more.

She moans, and I feel her warmth quiver around my shaft. I let go, and the release is intoxicating—halting my breath, my mind, and everything around me. I pour into her, and she digs her nails into my back. I love it. The moment couldn't be any more delicious.

After several long waves of release chase through me, I begin moving slowly, wringing out the last few shudders from her body before I collapse on top of her. Her breath is hard and fast, and I soak it in. The speed of her heart. The sugary smell of her sweat. The feeling of still being joined.

In four hundred years, I have never been with a woman and experienced this—sated yet so hungry for me.

"Oh my God, Michael," she pants, "that was amazing."

"Yes." I can't say more. I can hardly move.

"And did you *bite* me?"

"Yes." I kiss the spot at the side of her neck. "Just a little." To her it will appear like the smallest scratch. The hickey I just left on her is another story. *I hope she forgives me. And brought some makeup or a turtleneck.*

"Michael?"

"Yes."

"Can you…ummm…"

I lift my head and stare deeply into her chocolate-colored eyes, glossy with bliss. "Yes?"

"Can you...do that again?" she asks.

"It would be my pleasure." I seal my mouth over hers, knowing the flavor has cleared out. We start the dance all over again, and I savor every moment. I don't know what lies ahead, so I'll take the wins where I can get them.

CHAPTER TEN

Several hours later, I have made love to Miriam more times than I have with any woman. Or in the last century alone. Hey, do not judge me. As I said, sex lost its appeal after I turned one hundred. From time to time, I would feel the need and take care of things—plenty of women out there for a man like myself. But something was always lacking. Now I know what. A deeper connection.

I lay spooning her, both of us stretched across the narrow seat.

"Michael?" she says quietly.

"Yes?" I reply, thoroughly exhausted, but content for the first time I can ever recall. *Home* is the only word that comes to mind.

"I have a lot of questions."

"I thought you might," I whisper against the back of her neck.

"I'm not going to get pregnant, am I?"

I chuckle. It is a little late to be asking, but… "No. Not possible."

"Oh good. I saw that *Twilight* movie, and the girl gets knocked up by her vampire boyfriend."

"Complete fiction. Well, except for the day

walking and fast running. Also, we go insane if we do not sleep. We need downtime to keep our minds functioning properly."

"Oh." There's an awkward silence. "How did you become a vampire?"

I give her the short version, which comes down to getting a respiratory infection. I lived just outside London at the time in my family's home. My father, a merchant, had left with my mother to New Amsterdam, now New York City, to cash in on the settlers who were in need of building supplies, cooking utensils, and everything else one could imagine. I was left to be raised by a governess, servants, and, later, my professors at Cambridge. Clive was one of them, and we had an instant rapport—the father figure I always needed. Patient. Wise. Educated in the ways of the world.

"When I became ill, he could not stand to let me go. So he didn't," I say.

Still facing forward, Miriam sighs. "That is a sad but sweet story."

I leave out the part about how bitter I felt over what he did. I hadn't been the most religious man, but I did fear God. In my eyes, Clive made me into a demon. I spent a very long time coming to grips with what I was during my fur trapper/hunter days, but I eventually made my way back to Clive. That was when I learned there are two kinds of vampires: The ones who wanted to enslave humans like chattel, and those who wanted to live in peace and in secret. Things eventually came to a head between the two groups during the Great War.

"I think I need a drink to hear the rest of this." She sits up and twists around to look at me.

Her blonde hair is a hot mess, and her lips are swollen like two ripe berries from all of the kissing. I want to take a picture of her in this state so I can remember it always. *Idiot. Like you would ever forget.*

I hop up, slide on my jeans, and go to the back of the cabin. There is a small kitchenette and minifridge. I find a bottle of water and some of those tiny vodkas. Tucked in the door are some snack bars, so I grab one, too.

Miriam is dressing by the time I turn back toward her. I watch in silence, dumbfounded, as she covers her smooth round—

"Stop staring at my butt." She chuckles, but keeps her back to me.

"Not possible."

She slides up her jeans and puts on her blouse while I mourn the loss of the view. Those shoulders, the gentle curve of her thighs, the dip that runs the length of her spine, fading into the valley of the most perfect body part I've ever seen.

How is it possible I have never noticed the true beauty of a woman until now? Four hundred years old, and I feel like I am seeing it for the first time.

Miriam finishes dressing and takes a seat.

"Which do you prefer?" I sit beside her across the narrow aisle and hold out water in one hand, vodka in the other.

She grabs the water, guzzles it down, and then snatches the vodka. That, too, is gone in a second. I offer her the snack bar, but she declines. "I'm not hungry. Got any more water? And vodka?"

I retrieve them for her and watch them disappear.

"Better?"

"No." She shakes her head, keeping her eyes glued to the seat back in front of her.

"Trouble processing?" I retake my seat.

"Yes. Most definitely."

"Understandable," I reply and wait. This is not a moment to assert myself, and I know it. My true nature is a frightening thing to comprehend. My history, once I tell her the full story, might drive her to hate me. Hell, even I hate me for it, though I know I did what I had to. Someone had to be the Executioner. But that does not mean the faces do not haunt me, especially those of the children who weren't really children. Just monsters wearing masks, waiting to slaughter innocent people. Nevertheless, I felt no sense of victory after the war ended, and now I am questioning the point. What was it all for? Because here I am, three hundred years later, facing a collapse of everything I worked for.

"Are you really in love with me?" Miriam blurts out.

And point for the librarian, cutting straight to the

chase. My fearless bibliophile. "Yes." I look at her, but her eyes remain focused straight ahead. I do not mind. Whatever she needs to do to hear the truth.

"And the real reason for your creepy party?" she asks.

"I meant to perform the vampire wedding ceremony without your knowledge so that my soldiers will see you as an extension of myself and protect you."

"Marriage?" She turns her head, eyebrows raised.

"Yes."

"And why do I need the protection of soldiers?"

"We are about to go to war. The old regime wishes to reestablish itself."

"I'm assuming this would be a bad thing for people like me."

"Yes," I reply. "Very bad. They wish to return to the days when humans were treated as livestock."

"And Jeremy?" Her tiny hands grip the armrests of her chair. "You said he was a vampire too, but there's more to the story, isn't there?"

"He…" I whoosh out a breath.

"Tell me."

I want to protect her. It's in my nature to do so, and I do not care why, but now is not the time to hold back. She deserves the truth if we are to come out of this alive.

"He was one of them—the bad guys. He was there to try to win your trust and convince you to sell your land to those land developers."

Miriam scoffs. "Jeremy. What a...jerk."

"Basically, yes."

She shakes her head. "And here I've been crying myself to sleep every night."

"I'm sure he cared about you, Miriam. At least, to some extent. But they were merely after your land." I explain the blood farm, the catacombs, and how my maker was murdered to build a ruthless army.

"Holy cow." She looks out the window and sighs. "I guess I always suspected something was off with him and that whole situation. I mean, who tries to murder a librarian?"

"Monsters. This is why I killed the men they hired to hurt you."

She nods stoically. "Thank you."

"No thanks required. I did what was right."

She looks at me once again, her brown eyes filled with tears. "But you saved me, didn't you? The hospital. The attacks. The cult."

I nod.

"Not a cult at all," she concludes correctly. It dawns on me that while I have been working through my own mysteries, she has, too. I also realize that perhaps this "thing" between us is not so sudden after all. Since we've met, I've been there for her, protecting her, fighting for her. Those intelligent, observant eyes have been watching my every move. She may not have known my species, but she knows what sort of man I am.

"No," I finally confirm. "They were my council—the same ones now missing. They took us prisoner because they believed we were involved in the blood farm." Once I uncovered it, I ended up getting blamed. Our enemies took great care to frame me and cover their tracks.

"And you…you saved me again," she mutters.

I nod once more.

Miriam swallows hard and looks up at the ceiling, a few stray tears sliding from the corners of her eyes. "From the first moment we met, I knew something was different."

"I felt the same. It is why I stayed when you thought I was there to interview—"

"No. Sorry. I meant Jeremy. When we met, there was something strange about him. But then…I don't know. We spent more time together, and I honestly felt like he cared. There was this vibe though, like he resented what he felt."

As I listen, Miriam's words hit several chords: jealousy, anger, bitterness. I may not understand our connection, but I would never use her like that.

"Well," I say, "I am sorry, but Jeremy was not a good man. Not good at all, and if you and I want to survive the mess he helped create, then we will need to stick together."

"Absolutely." She straightens her spine. "I'm all in. What's the game plan?"

Hold on. "Miriam, why aren't you looking for

the nearest rock to hide under?" Again, she seems to be taking this rather well.

"You honestly think that little of me, after I just let you—a vampire—bang me and fang me for three hours?"

Errr...okeydokey. "No?"

"Good. Because I am not some...some delicate little bookworm who's going to cower in the self-help section. Whoever these horrible people—or ex-people—are, I'm not letting them mess with the world I love."

"Wow. I do not think I could possibly be more turned on than I am right now."

"Really?"

"Oh yes."

"Good. Because I'm ready for more." She flashes a greedy little grin.

Dear God. What is this woman made of? Carbon fiber steel? Kryptonite? "I must rest, Miriam. If I do not, I will become too hungry."

"Then eat." She tilts her head to the side and flashes a bit of yummy vein. "I don't mind."

"No." I lean back. "Put that away. What I did to you before was...well, foreplay. When I'm hungry, it is not the same."

"So, you're saying you would kill me?"

"No. Never. But why wave a credit card in front of a shopaholic?"

"Michael, am I safe around you or not?" she asks.

I am tired of the lies and deceptions, but more than anything, I need Miriam to trust me. "You are safe up to a point, but is that not the same for regular humans?"

"Huh?"

"Well, people have been known to eat other people in situations where they were starving."

"Ewww."

"Absolutely, but it is true." I shrug.

"So, basically, you *could* decide to eat me if we were plane wrecked in the Himalayas?"

"No. Not even then. I would take my own life before I would ever allow myself to get that hungry." I know she is now thinking about the time we were held captive by "the cult," locked up together in a coffin. Long story short, the council wanted to see what we knew about the blood farm and decided a little torture was in order. I surmised we could be there for days or weeks, and I would grow hungry. I decided to end my life instead of allowing myself to harm her. I failed, of course.

"Okay. Let's move," she says. "Tell me what we need to do."

"What do you mean, *we?*"

"I just told you; I'm not going to sit around, waiting for a bunch of immortal thugs to gang-rape the human race."

I shirk. "It's more of a mass enslavement, but either way, you are not equipped for this."

She narrows her eyes. "Michael Vanderhorst,

you might be a vampire, but I am still your boss, and I am not taking no for an answer. How can I help?"

I quickly explain how the council members have been taken and we must free them. The societies, all five hundred and eighty-two, still have leaders in place, but those leaders lack the seniority and clout to unite an entire region. Their jobs are to manage their territories and follow orders. Without our councils to enforce things, it's going to be left up to me and the generals to lead.

Miriam's eyes are wide with shock. "They took all of the council members?"

"Yes. However, Nice was with them and set free. I do not know why, but either way, I must decide how to rescue them."

"Didn't you say you're some great general from a big war?"

"Yes."

"Then why in the world are you putting your eggs in that basket? I mean, come on. I've never fought a day in my life, and even I can see that rescuing these council members is a nonstarter. Total trap."

I cannot answer her question honestly because that would require I explain in detail the things I had to do in the last war. It is far too disturbing, far too grim. So while she has taken all of the news I've delivered thus far like a champ, this is different.

"I fought one war, Miriam. I fought so much

that my soul bled, and I lost every piece of me that was worth a damn." I exhale. "And then I met you. Three hundred years later. Three hundred years of sleepwalking through the day and reliving my sins each night. After all that I gave, all that I have been through, I cannot—I will not return to that shell of a man. Not when I feel alive again."

"Oh." Miriam blinks. "Then yeah. We really gotta rescue your council members. What's left of them. By the way, did I thank you for saving me from Nice?"

"You did."

"Good. Because I really, really hope that from here on out, Michael, these games are over. I mean, I know I was the one who didn't want to listen, but that's done. Oh. Ver."

I grin at her. "Nothing could please me more."

Miriam chuckles and runs a hand through her frazzled hair, like she's keeping a little joke to herself.

"What?" I ask.

"Nothing."

"No more secrets, remember?" I push.

She shakes her head. "It's just…I had this crazy grandfather everyone used to talk about. I never met him, but he always came up at family gatherings. Crazy Grandpa Kipper."

"What did they say about him?" I smile in anticipation of an amusing story.

"Besides being crazy?"

"Obviously."

Miriam shrugs. "He told everyone he was a vampire hunter. He claimed they were every-where—the post office, the grocery store, mowing his lawn. They said he naturally drew them in. Anyway, he had to be locked up because he kept throwing holy water on people to check if they were human. The last straw was when he filled his house with chocolate and began making little frozen chocolate pellets to shoot from a slingshot he made. He nearly killed a census taker."

What. The. What? "What makes you think he was crazy?" Because I truly hope she's right. This could be bad.

"Michael, he just was. I mean, the man thought he had something in his blood that lured vampires in so he could kill them. And he thought everyone was a vampire. I mean…everyone."

Holy frozen chocolate balls.

She goes on. "It's just a coincidence, I'm sure, but imagine Grandpa Kipper's face if he learned vampires were actually real. And that toilets really can speak—the Japanese ones anyway."

"The toilet?"

"Oh yeah. Sometimes the dishwasher and clothes hamper were in on it." She sighs. "Poor guy. He passed away in a mental institution. My mom never quite got over it."

I refrain from smiling, but on the inside, I'm all grins. For a moment, I thought Miriam was telling me that her grandfather was one of these…these…Oh, hell. What was the name? I cannot recall, but Clive mentioned them once many years ago when he attempted to explain how he and the other eleven vampires were made. Something about counterweights. I asked what that meant, but he never gave me an answer. He simply said that our evolution was a random act of nature, but that didn't mean we could be trusted to act in nature's best interest.

Thank God that Miriam's grandfather was just a loon. I hope? *No. She is not a chocolate-slinging vampire killer.*

Miriam sighs. "The strange thing is, I once overheard my parents talking in the study. My mom said she felt like she was being watched. That's when my dad upgraded the security system and added the fence."

My mind starts filling with doubt. What if there is something in her blood, an attractant of sorts? It would explain why I am—

No. Not possible. I want Miriam because she is beautiful and unique, I tell myself. But now the seed has been planted.

"Are you all right?" Miriam asks.

"Of course."

"Then why do you look like you've just seen a ghost? Or a talking hamper?" She smiles, but it doesn't touch her eyes.

"I am truly fine. I simply do not know what to

do with you—how to keep you safe while I assess the situation with our council members."

"What was your original plan?" she asks.

"Put on an appropriate disguise and do a little reconnaissance at the pits, including determining what sort of facility is built over them today."

"This plane got Wi-Fi?"

I nod.

She gets up, grabs her backpack, which I'd left on a seat toward the front, and returns with her phone. She taps the device with her finger. "Where are these pits located?"

"About ten miles directly east of Blackpool, England."

"Ah." She bobs her head. "And now I see why you made up the story about the uncle with the books. You wanted to go to Liverpool to look into this whole thing."

"I'm sorry for the deception. If it makes you feel any better, there actually is a collection—quite old and belonging to my family, though it is probably turned to dust by now."

"Considering the circumstances, I can forgive you for lying, Michael, but not for letting good books go to waste."

"Truly unforgivable." I simply hadn't had the motivation to care for anything belonging to my parents. I hardly knew them. Odd how I never did let their things go, however.

Miriam hands me her phone. "Use the satellite

map feature."

It takes a moment to realize what she is saying. "I suppose I could have done that to begin with. You are a smart woman." I can see what occupies the pits today.

Still seated, I zoom in on the image, but the area is all grazing fields. One particular spot is covered with trees. "I think this actually might be the place. The tree line forms a perfect circle, but I find it hard to believe the pits would have been left open."

"Maybe they're not. Maybe they're covered to look like pastures."

"Maybe. But I don't like it."

"Like what?" she asks.

"This hardly seems like a secure enough location to hold such valuable prisoners." I had imagined the pits might be below a home or building. At the very least, they'd be covered by a barn.

Mystery! Mystery! Mystery!

Shut up. Nobody's speaking to you.

"I think it sounds like the perfect spot to hide something," Miriam says. "In plain sight. Middle of nowhere."

Don't you dare, inner-vampire-child mystery junky. I check the time. We should be right over New York City. We could stop here or stay the course. On one hand, Miriam is right; going to rescue the council members is a risk—not that I would be doing it alone. If I find them there, I would have to trust Otto and his men to assist. On the other hand, what if Nice and Miriam are right? This could be a trap. *Or not.*

"I will tell the pilot to continue on to Liverpool," I say. "From there, I will travel to the pits. You will stay in the plane and wait for me."

"Ha. No. If you're going to the pits, I'm going with you. To the pits." She pauses. "Can we rename them? Every time I say 'the pits,' I imagine myself feeling depressed, sitting on the sofa, binging on pork rinds and *Heart of Dixie.*"

Ick...pork rinds. Heart of Dixie, however, I can get behind. Lula got me hooked. That, and *Vampire Diaries.* Hysterical. As if we'd go around crying all the time like that Claus man. *So unrealistic.* "Miriam, I am sorry, but you must stay on the plane. I am not going to risk your safety or negotia—"

"You're not my husband, daddy, or any other figure with power over me. Not that my husband would have power over me, but you understand."

"This is not about power." I shake my head. "It is simply too dangerous."

She takes the seat across the aisle and grabs my hand. "Michael, I thought I made myself clear. This world is my home, too. I'm not going to sit on my butt and do nothing. So we're in this together now. Also, I'm probably safer with you than anywhere else if you're not sure who to trust."

She has a point. "Very well, but I am in charge."

She laughs.

"Miriam, this is not a joke. These vampires are

dangerous."

"I don't doubt it."

"Then why are you making light?" I ask.

"How can you not 'make light'? This is the most insane, improbable situation ever. It belongs in a movie or as a storyline for Fanged Love. But it's not a fantasy, Michael. You're a vampire. I'm a librarian. We are looking at the end of the world if we don't do something." She throws her hands in the air. "Does it get any weirder than that?"

"No. And I have seen much weirdness."

"Exactly. And the strangest thing of all? I feel like I've been preparing for this my entire life—like I was meant to do this."

I am stunned. Never in a million years would I have guessed that Miriam could handle this so well. I guess Lula was right. Miriam is much more resilient than I gave her credit for. Just one more sign that we are meant to be together.

Suddenly, there is that nagging in the back of my mind again. What if I'm wrong?

CHAPTER ELEVEN

By the time we land in Liverpool, it is almost five p.m. with the time zone difference, and Miriam is just waking up. I've made a few phone calls, including to Lula and Viviana, who are hunkered down, but hard at work making inquiries with other societies and their leaders.

The strange part is, there has been no action taken by our enemies. No attacks. No soldiers. No suspicious activities reported whatsoever. In other words, something just isn't right. I would have expected them to make a move by now before our side has time to get our act together. Strike while the iron is hot.

It simply doesn't add up. So at this point, the only thing we know for certain is that everyone is on edge. Something is coming, something big, yet how can we prepare when we are flying blind?

Speaking of flying…

"You're all set, sir," says Fernando. "I'll have the plane fueled up and ready to go when you get back."

"Thank you. You're a good man," I say, putting together the last of my disguise. I have on a black helmet with spikes, a biker outfit complete with chaps and a fishnet shirt, and dark sunglasses. My fake goatee is purple for that extra flair, and, of course, I have bathed myself in Jovan Musk.

"Michael? What the hell?" Miriam's bloodshot eyes crack open. "Why are you dressed like a leather daddy? With a purple beard?" She pinches her nose. "And what is that smell? It's making me dizzy."

"Only because I used a gallon of it. Didn't want it to wear off before we arrive to our destination." I toss a shopping bag into the seat next to her.

"What is that?" She glances at the bag.

"That's Lula's disguise. She's a few sizes larger than you, but it should still fit. And did I mention we're taking a motorcycle?"

Miriam pulls out the black leather short-shorts and matching vest. "I am not wearing this."

"We cannot simply drive up on someone's property dressed as ourselves."

"But—but that outfit is—"

"Sexy, and you have always desired to wear it while sitting on a Harley and strapped to a sexy dangerous vampire?" I joke.

"Errr…"

"Stick with me, and I will make all of your fantasies come to life."

"I'll go get changed." She slides past me into the bathroom. Fernando simply stands there giving me a look.

"What?" I ask.

"I am finding it difficult to believe you are our

king."

I do appear rather goofy. "I am really more of a suit man. I believe it is the proper attire of a gentleman."

"I was actually thinking how tame you are. Have you seen what Nice wears on official business trips or holidays?"

"Do I want to know?"

"Not unless you're into baby doll dresses and parasols for grown men."

"Then that would be a no."

"Well, I wish you all the luck. Call if you need anything."

"Thank you, friend," I reply.

I have arranged for the local rental agency to have the motorcycle parked outside, and the keys left in the private airport's office. After a brief visit with the local immigration officials, we will be on our way. I only hope they do not give me any headaches over my outfit.

Miriam steps out of the bathroom, and I feel my pulse quicken. Her shorts are more like leather panties, and her tight vest doesn't leave much to the imagination.

My tongue falls from my mouth. "I beg of you to consider making that your new librarian outfit. I think it would really do wonders to inspire more books to be checked out."

"Yeah, no. Shall we go?" she asks cheerily.

Miriam seems too at ease for such a dangerous

mission. We do not know what we will find. *But at least if she is dressed like that, I will go happy if anything happens.*

Forty minutes later, we are riding down a back road toward Blackpool, the foggy afternoon wind whipping through our leather garments. Miriam is holding me so tight I can barely breathe.

"Ease up there, Miriam. You're going to break me."

"There aren't any seatbelts back here. You're the next best thing!" she yells over the loud motor.

I must admit, she is taking everything in stride, including a small hiccup at the airport. Apparently, they suspected us of being in some rock group and failing to obtain the proper work visas—the downside of flying in a private jet and looking so glamorous. However, my worries are only increasing. Our enemy's radio silence and Miriam's disclosure about her grandfather are perturbing, though completely unrelated. Still, doubt has settled in my bones, and I find myself wondering if everything I'm doing is wrong, including pursuing a relationship with Miriam. What if my feelings for her are a chemical reaction to some potent, vampire-attracting pheromone? It would be unfair and ungentlemanly to continue with her until I know for certain.

I take a turn down a narrow road lined with green fields and grazing cattle. Up ahead to the right is a barn and what appears to be an unworked farm. I do not know who might be watching, so I have warned Miriam to put on a good show.

I nudge her with my elbow—the signal.

"Oh. Gotcha. Hey, Miguel," she yells, "I gotta pee real bad. Can you find some big tall trees so I can go?" Her words come out robotic and stale.

Someone needs acting lessons if they're going to be my sidekick. "Sure, babe! I'll pull in right here and find you a good spot for a tinkle."

"You're the best, sugar."

We make our way past several more run-down farms—dilapidated barns, driveways overrun with weeds—until I spot the location of the pits. I pull over and hit the kickstand.

"Honey, can you keep a lookout?" She hops off the back.

"Sure thing, sweetie pie." I follow her toward the tree line, listening for any sounds, including a shift in the density of the soil. If there are tunnels beneath us or a hatch of any sort, then my heavy leather boots will help me find them.

We approach, and I am on my guard, ready for anything.

"What the…" *All right. I was not ready for this.*

"Is that why the town is called Blackpool?" Miriam asks.

I scratch my head and stare down at the water.

What was once an open pit is now a dark, murky duck pond.

"I do not understand." I turn on my heel, wondering if I miscalculated the spot. I see a hill off in the distance at the exact location I remember from long, long ago. The beach is directly west a few miles.

We need to get out of here. "Had a good pee, honey?" I say loudly. "Let's hit the road."

We casually walk back to the bike, but on the inside, my inner detective is yelling at me: *You suck! You couldn't solve your way out of a granny knot.*

We mount the bike and hit the road again. We have been sent on a wild-goose chase for sure. And it was Nice who sent us on it. But why?

Wait. He was the one who said not to come, that it was a trap. On the other hand, I cannot trust him. Especially not after he flipped out and tried to steal Miriam.

Several miles down the road, I pull over and call Lula. "Anything happening? Anything at all?"

"No. Why?"

"Because the pits are ponds. Nice lied to us."

"Seriously? Wow. I honestly don't have a clue, Michael. Just be careful and keep me posted."

"Will do." I end the call and dial Otto, but it goes into voicemail. In all my years, Otto has never *not* answered. Not even when we used telegraphs. He would dot-dot-dash back within the hour, the fastest one could hope for back then.

Sonofabiscuit. There are two global headquarters, one here and one in Wellington, Kansas. I have no clue how they chose these locations—some sort of fan raffle, I imagine. But I call the Blackpool switchboard first. No answer. *This is not good.* I call Wellington, and it too goes unanswered.

Crap. I groan.

"It's bad news, isn't it?" Miriam asks.

I am tempted to make something up in order to spare her the worry, but I want Miriam to trust me, and there are no excuses for my lies. Not anymore. She deserves to hear the full truth, and the last twenty-four hours have proven she can handle it. The problem now seems to be with me. My four-century-old brain cannot quite figure out what is happening.

"Yes. It is bad news." We get back on the road, heading in the direction of the airport.

With the wind in my hair, my purple goatee flapping against my cheek, and a scantily clad librarian pressed to my back, I have never felt more out of control than I do in this very moment. I am driving blind and everything is at stake.

Stop the pity party, Vanderhorst. You survived the Great War. You have lived through many more wars since then and witnessed the birth of a great nation. You helped make this world a better place. You have lived a life of honor, always seeking wisdom and to help others. "I can do this."

"What?" Miriam screams. "I can't hear you!"

"Nothing," I yell back. "I was just thinking about what my maker Clive would tell me if he were alive."

"Yeah? What's that?" she bellows back.

"He would say something like trust your instincts, look at the least obvious answers, assume everyone is trying to..." My words fade with the blades of grass passing us by. My heart tumbles to the asphalt beneath us. My soul quakes. I am suddenly back in that small room beside his lecture hall three hundred eighty years ago, drinking wine and talking to him. I am young, strong, healthy, and alive. He is the first person I have ever met who has earned my respect and trust.

"Michael, excuse me if I speak out of turn," he said, "but you, sir, are a brave talker and nothing more. You spout off about wanting to see the world and learn everything, yet you do not wish to confront the ugliness of life."

"I have had my fair share of ugliness, I assure you." My wealthy parents left me behind to make an even bigger fortune in the New World. I was raised by uncaring, strict servants who would beat me if I stepped out of line. Years later, they would become my first meals.

"That is not what I mean," responded Clive. "You have a good nature, but it allows others to deceive you."

I chuckled. "I think not."

"Hear my words, Vanderhorst. You take everyone at face value. But if you want to be the master of your own destiny, you must look beyond what your eyes show you. Learn to trust your gut."

A few weeks later, I would discover the true meaning of his words. He was a vampire who drank blood for sustenance. I would become his first protégé.

As Miriam and I drive back to the airport, my mind reluctantly runs through the maze in search of cheese. There are only two people who have ever truly known me inside and out, who could predict my moves and know how I think. One is dead: Clive. The other is Lula. But I have been down this path before, believing she has betrayed me, only to find she has risked life and limb to save me.

There has to be another answer.

Miriam and I pull into the parking lot of the private airport, and I help her dismount.

"You okay, Michael?"

No. Not even a little. "Sure." I take her hand and guide her to the office where we must declare our departure. This time, they do not mistake us for anything but a strange couple who doesn't know how to dress properly.

Within forty-five minutes, we are on the plane and up in the air. My mind runs wild with questions, hypothetical answers, and everything implausible that lies in between.

Miriam sits quietly beside me. I wonder if she can feel my stress or just sees the obvious signs.

Either way, she knows something is up.

Having quickly changed into jeans and my light blue button-down, I slide the phone from my pocket and call Lula.

"Mike! Anything new?" she asks.

"No."

"Really? That's not good."

"No."

"Hmmm…you heading back?" she asks.

"Change of plans. I've been in touch with all the generals. We're setting up a meeting to figure this out together. I do not see another way." This is not true, of course, but I must know what Lula will say. It is a horrible idea and anyone with half a brain would say so. *Didn't stop Otto from suggesting it.*

"Great! Where's the meeting? I'll join you," she says.

Wrong answer. If Lula were truly on my side, she would be telling me I'm a fool for gathering our military leaders in one place.

Dammit, Lula. Are you really in on this? I can't believe it. I don't want to.

My heart suddenly feels heavy. In this moment, the only one I can trust is Miriam, and the irony is that I don't trust what we have.

"Lula, I'm sorry, but I must put my foot down. You are safe right now, and that is all I can ask for."

"Silly, you can ask for more than that. We're a team. Tell me where you're going, you shit, or I swear I'll never forgive you. Because you and I both know a room full of generals can't make any decisions without a smart girl present."

"I'll text you the information," I lie.

"Mikey?" Lula says.

"Yes?" I reply.

"You know that you're everything to me, don't you?"

Her words spear me right in the heart.

"I do," I lie again.

"Good. Because whatever happens, I want you to know I am behind you."

Sonofabitch. Yes, yes, there I go again, swearing, but this time it is warranted. Lula is never that nice. She is definitely hiding something.

I know what I must do. I look over at Miriam. It's just me and her now. The entire human race and the majority of decent vampires are depending on a librarian and her assistant to figure this out and save them.

Well, at least *she* is smart.

CHAPTER TWELVE

I know my feelings for Miriam are unresolved, no matter how real they seem, but at least she can be trusted. So when I explain my hypothesis to her about something bigger, uglier going on, she doesn't flinch.

"Yeah. Well, it all fits. But why would Lula decide to betray you now, after everything she's done to help you?"

"I cannot imagine, but if you come up with an explanation, I'm all ears."

"Nope. I'm still trying to understand how you require human blood to stay alive."

"Our kind lacks certain nutrients due to our state of semi-suspended animation—a result of a virus that slows down our circulatory systems and makes it so that our cells require minimal amounts of oxygen, which means our DNA does not deteriorate as quickly, but also leaves major organs depleted of essential nutrients because of slower blood flow. I studied the phenomena for the last decade in my bioengineering job—after hours, of course. But do not worry. The virus itself is not a very hardy strain. It requires ideal conditions in order to transfer to a new host. Might I say, it is the eight-track of communicable diseases. Not nearly as sophisticated as an Ebola or AIDS virus, for example. The orchid of viruses for all intents and purposes." I look at Miriam, who blinks rapidly.

"Nerd alert."

I frown. "Yes, well…I take my work seriously."

"Are all vampires as anal retentive as you when it comes to work?"

"Yes. And no. Whatever we endeavor, we tend to obsess over it. For example, Jiffy, a vampire who belongs to my society in Arizona, excels at naps and eating peanut butter, but there is no one better, more dedicated to his craft."

Miriam laughs. "Sorry I asked."

"Do not be. You can ask me anything."

She looks away, out the small window at the late evening sky.

"Is there something else you wish to ask?" I question.

"It's a little silly."

"Makes it all the more appropriate for a vampire," I say.

She turns her head back to me. "Were you excited to marry me?"

"That's a question I do not know how to answer."

"Why?" she asks.

"I never considered the marriage to be real."

"Did you want it to be?"

Yes. Absolutely. But… "What sort of idiot sets himself up for such disappointment?"

"The kind who's in love. Or did you not mean what you said earlier?"

I no longer know if what I feel is true, and I won't until I get to the bottom of this thing about her grandfather. "I planned to marry you in order to secure the protection of my army. Beyond that, everything I hoped for was inconsequential."

She nods. "I guess I understand."

"If we had married, how would you feel right now?" I ask.

She shrugs. "I'm not sure. I…I have issues. I'm sure you've noticed my lack of close friends."

I nod. "You fear losing them."

"Something like that. I mean, I know that death is a natural part of life. I would argue it makes life precious. But there's something about a tragic death before a person's time that jars you. I think it's why we see it on the news or worry about it happening to the people we love. No one ever says, 'Well, hey, he was going to die in fifty years anyway. Guess it's better to get it over with.'"

"No." I chuckle. "Certainly not."

"But with you, I'm not so afraid."

"You like the fact I'm so durable," I guess.

"Is that weird or rude?" She crinkles her nose. It's cute.

"Not at all. But I wonder…"

"What?" she asks.

"If my durable nature is what drove you to give yourself to me."

She looks away.

"We are being honest, are we not?" I prod.

She inhales and gazes deeply into my eyes. "No. I wanted you from the first moment we met, and I feel ashamed about it."

I chuckle bemusedly.

"Stop it," she scolds. "It's not funny. I felt like a complete pervert."

"Dear God, woman. I am not a child. Nor do I look like one."

"Yeah, but I pushed you to take the job, and I knew you weren't there for an interview." I wandered in, wearing a suit—my preferred clothing—and she let on like I was there for the assistant's position. I played along, and now I wonder if it was because of this vampire attractant.

But the attractant would not affect her *feelings. So at least there's that.* "Are you saying your intentions were dishonorable and that you meant to take advantage of my innocent body from day one? Shocking. How do you live with yourself?"

"You're pissing me off now, Mike."

I raise my hands. "Apologies." I can't help but smile despite her irritation. "But you do understand the irony, yes? I am older than most countries."

"Now I do, but at the time, I thought there was something wrong with me. Who hires a guy so they can look at their ass? Or have fantasies of seducing them? It's just not me. Especially since I had a boyfriend at the time."

I personally love hearing that this entire time she was lusting after me as much as I was her. "Do not feel bad. You never acted on your attraction while you were with him, and the last time I checked, fantasizing is not a crime."

As I'm basking in the glow of inappropriate workplace romances, I think again of the fact that perhaps none of it is real—at least for me—even if I feel it.

"So, now that we've cleaned out our dirty little secrets," she says, "what are we going to do about it?"

I wish I knew. "For the moment, we have bigger issues."

"You mean your missing council members or the people who aren't returning your calls?"

"All of the above, but," I shake my head, "I think the matter at hand is much worse than I could have anticipated. They have outsmarted us. Outmaneuvered us. I am a king without an army. A man without a plan."

"Come on. You're saying the war is over? There hasn't even been a battle yet."

"Possibly," I reply.

"But you can't give up like that."

"You think I want to?" I retort, feeling the full force of my frustration.

"No, but I think you're doing it anyway."

"If it makes you feel better, I plan to go check on Lula and Viviana. Then we can give up. Maybe we find a chalet in the Alps. Perhaps we go underground and begin planning a resistance. They may be able to defeat me, but there are over seven billion humans on the planet. Vampires can never rule them all."

"I don't like your plan. It sucks."

"Agreed, but it does not change our next step and that you should put your disguise back on— merely a precaution."

"Again?" she asks.

"I do not want to risk being spotted when we land." I stifle a smile.

She laughs. "You just want to see me in those shorts again!"

"Can you blame me?"

"There'll be time for sexy dress-up when this is all over. In the meantime, I'm going back to comfy sweaters and skirts."

I smile weakly. I like that she is optimistic that this "will all be over" and end favorably, because I am not so sure.

᚛ ᚜

Thirty hours after our trip began, Fernando has taken us right back where we started, to the private airport just outside Phoenix. I can only hope he is truly on my side, as I was for him over two hundred years ago, when I taught him to fight, to track, and how to pass off one's self as human. With that knowledge, he trained others and played a key part in the Civil War. I am ashamed to admit it, but I did not fight by his side. By then I was far too damaged from the Great War to even look at a battlefield. Instead, I moved to Virginia and opened a barbershop. Yes, that's right. I even faked a limp and an accent so no one would question why a young man of twenty wasn't fighting alongside his Confederate brothers. Oddly, it was a peaceful time in my life. I would cut hair and shave beards of the men too old to fight. They were like hens who gossiped day and night. Anything of interest I heard, I passed along to Fernando. At night, I would go to the encampments behind the front lines and pick off captains, generals, or anyone who looked tasty and might be of strategic value, but I never fought.

After the Civil War, I moved to Ohio and opened a new barbershop, where I would stay until Clive's return in the early 1900s. One day, he told me he was opening a detective agency, and I was in. The problem was that while our societies were established and fully functioning by then, there was still a lack of cooperation between territories. Clive and I filled that gap—looking for missing persons, helping business owners when shipments of product went missing in another society's territory, and keeping tabs on roving packs of vampires who had refused to come into the fold. Eventually, toward the end of the century, I had to find other work because Clive couldn't afford to pay me. As I mentioned, our cover stories in the human world must look authentic, and his business had been losing money. I certainly did not need the paycheck, but on paper, Clive was going bankrupt. At the time, I simply scratched my head. Why would he run his business like a charity? I would call him a softy or irresponsible, but that was Clive, always trying to make the world a better place.

The plane slows to a crawl and then pulls into a spot next to the hangar. I am vigilant, looking for any sign of Nice, soldiers, anything. But it is just after four in the morning, and all I hear are crickets and the faint sounds of cars passing on the main thoroughfare.

I grab my things and prepare to disembark.

"This is where we part ways, old friend," Fernando says. "I must return to my society and check on everyone."

He now oversees Georgia. It's quite the busy little territory, with many vampires coming and going for business, but he has five deputies to assist.

"Thank you for everything." I shake his hand.

"I am always here for you, Vanderhorst."

Miriam says goodbye, but waits for me at the top of the stairs so I can do a quick sweep of the surrounding area. I had planned on grabbing an Uber just outside the airport, but I see the electric boogaloo has been left in the parking lot.

I walk over. *Keys are still inside. Glad to see they're cautious sorts around here*, I think sarcastically.

I scan the buildings around us and listen carefully. Not a sound. Not a breath. Not even a breeze. Still, the hairs on the back of my neck stand straight up.

"Hurry. Let's go." I wave her over.

Miriam takes the stairs and walks to my car, but doesn't get inside. Instead, she simply stands next to the passenger door with a strange look in her eyes, like she's mulling something over.

"What are you waiting for?" I whisper across the roof.

"Michael, you still haven't told me the plan."

"Stay alive. That's my plan."

"I'm serious. You say you want to check on Lula and Viviana. Then what?" she asks.

"I am still thinking."

"Well then, while you do that, I want to go home."

What happened to doing this together? "Home? You cannot go home. Not until this is over. Perhaps not ever."

"I'm not leaving my books, Michael."

"So you are proposing to stay here and be a lamb for the slaughter?" I do not like that plan.

"I understand what you're saying, but if this huge wave of bloodthirsty vampires is coming to take us all out, I'd rather stand and fight."

"You just really don't want to leave your books

behind," I presume.

"They're everything to me, Michael."

"You're willing to die protecting a bunch of books?" I ask.

"Uh, yeah. Books. Hello...?"

I want to roll my eyes, but I do not. "They are merely things. They can be replaced. You cannot."

"Bite your tongue. Books are not just things. And these particular ones are my family's legacy. Generations of Murphys have worked and slaved and hunted for each book in this collection with the sole purpose of keeping them safe for generations to come."

"And I am sure they will be quite *safe* locked up inside your home," I argue.

"What if someone burns my house down? What if this war happens, and I can't go back home? Not ever?"

"We cannot run around hauling millions of books. We would need fifty U-Hauls—"

"Then at least let me retrieve my mother's ring. It's a priceless family heirloom, and she gave it to me on my eighteenth birthday. Please, Michael? It belonged to my great-great-grandmother. I can't part with it."

Christ. She lost her mother and father last year, so denying her something of such sentimental value would be heartless, but that does *not* change the facts.

"Miriam," I say in my most sympathetic voice,

"we do not have time. I must go and see Lula and Viviana." I need to look Lula in the eyes and hear her say she is truly on our side, because I cannot accept she would betray me. It simply does not make sense after everything we've been through. Then we must all get out of Dodge.

"Fine," Miriam throws back, "you go check on them, and I'll take a cab back to my place. We can meet there."

"Nice might be waiting for you. The enemy's soldiers might be waiting," I argue.

"Then *you* take me to get my ring."

Stubborn little librarian. Why won't she listen to reason? "Standing about is unsafe. Let's discuss this in the car."

"Nope." She crosses her arms. "Not until we're in agreement."

I lose my patience—I am, after all, still a vampire. We have short fuses. "Get in the *caca azul*, woman. A war is coming, and I do not have time to debate."

She gives me a look. "You really call your car the blue shit?"

"Among many different names, yes. And you will ride in it."

"I am not one of your soldiers, Mike. Oh, sorry. *King* Mike. You don't get to tell me what to do."

I groan. She knows I hate being called Mike. "Would you *please*," I growl, "pretty please get in the *caca azul*?"

"Agree to take me by my place, and I'll get in the car. It will only take two minutes. In and out of the vault, and we're done."

The vault? I have been dying to see what's in there.

No. No. That is no reason to take a detour. I look her in the eyes and note the despair. *But her feelings are.* "All right. But we will have to be quick about it."

CHAPTER THIRTEEN

Every minute of the drive to Miriam's house, I'm expecting something to happen—Nice to pop out from behind a tree and jump on the hood, our car to be surrounded by a caravan of armored SUVs, or to get pulled over by a police officer, only to find he or she is an imposter and we are forced to fight.

I can protect myself. I can fight like no one else. But I cannot do it while keeping Miriam safe. My kind is simply too fast, and if there are more than one, she will be easy pickings.

Despite my jumpiness, we arrive to Miriam's front door without issue.

"Well, that's a good sign." Miriam punches a code into the console in the foyer. "Nothing's been triggered."

"Let us hurry. I need to stop by my disguise locker."

"You have a storage locker just for that?" She stifles a smile.

"Of course. One never knows when they will need a cowboy hat or hook nose."

"Wait. Were you there the night Jeremy died?"

Oh boy. I forgot about that. It was the night of

the party where the vampires who were running the blood farm, which included Jeremy and his boss, held their auction. They had actually taken Lula prisoner and were planning to sell her blood to the highest bidder. *Eternal life could be yours for just a cool million.* I showed up dressed as cowboy Frank, one of my best costumes, posing as a bidder. I saved Lula, and the party was shut down, as were the humans who knew too much, but Jeremy and his boss ran, taking Miriam with them. When we caught up, the two men were already dusted. Miriam saw the whole thing, though she'd been heavily drugged.

"I was there that night," I admit. "And I'm sorry I didn't get the chance to explain."

"Did you kill Jeremy?"

"No. I believe it was one of Alex's men. They saw my disguise and used a similar outfit. The people behind all this wanted fingers pointed towards me—the blood farm, the party, the cover-up."

"Oh." Miriam nods solemnly and lets out a sigh. "Well, it was a really great disguise." Her tone lacks any color.

Still standing in her foyer, I take her hand and give it a squeeze. "I'm sorry you had to go through that. But more than anything, I'm sorry that Jeremy turned out to be so unworthy of you. No woman deserves to be misled and used in such a manner. Especially you, Miriam."

She looks up at me, her eyes glassy. "Do you really mean that, Michael?"

"Of course."

"Then why do I sense something's wrong?" Her tone is soft and vulnerable. "You've hardly looked at me since Blackpool."

I do not want to tell her what I'm thinking because I do not know if it is real. Does she have something inside her that attracts me subconsciously, or am I in love with her? Does it even matter? All I know is that telling her the truth will hurt her, and for what? It could be complete bullcrap.

"I am simply overwhelmed by the puzzling situation," I say. "I do not see a good way through this."

"Is that why you're not making a real plan?" she asks. "Or is there another reason?"

"What do you mean? I have a plan. Retreat."

"All right. Let me rephrase. Are you unable to take the bull by the horns because you're too afraid something will happen to me?"

I look down at my shoes, giving it some thought. "Yes. Perhaps so." Fear is like a cancer to a clear mind. It blocks you from seeing the truth and taking action. It is poison.

"I see." She bobs her head. "So I'm holding you back."

"I do not view it that way. You are in this mess because of me, and it is my duty to keep you safe."

She shakes her head in disagreement. "If you didn't have to worry about protecting me, you'd probably be off right now hunting down these evil vampires instead of wanting to go into hiding. Yes or no?"

I nod but do not speak.

"Wow. Okay." She whistles out a breath. "Then I need to find a really safe place so you can get to work."

"I am not sure there is one." And I do not like the idea of Miriam leaving my side.

"I inherited my parents' cabin. It's two hours north of here in Flagstaff. My mother used to go up there a lot in the summers to escape the heat."

"If there are public records, anyone can find it." Her family also owned a hacienda about an hour south of the city. I believe Miriam put it up for sale recently to help pay taxes on her home since her library doesn't bring in much money—just the occasional book sale or two. That said, when Jeremy and his boss took Miriam after that auction, we tracked them down to her hacienda by using public records.

"But the cabin is still in my mother's maiden name," she argues. "She inherited the property from my grandparents before she met my father. It wouldn't be so easy to trace back to me."

That does make sense. "I think you would be safe, at least for a few days. I can take you there now." I only wish I could send someone I trust with her, but there is no one.

"Great. Let's go get my ring. I'll also grab a few

supplies from the kitchen."

We pass through Miriam's enormous skating-rink-sized living room and take a set of spiral stairs into the basement. There are several doors, likely utility closets, lining the long hallway.

We arrive to a solid-looking door with a keypad. *Here it is. The infamous vault.* She's hinted at the many book treasures down here, and I am a sucker for such things.

She punches in some numbers, and the lock pops. With a push, we're inside another hallway, but this one is lined with glass cabinets.

"I keep some of our more valuable things in this temperature-controlled room," she says, "but the priceless stuff is in there." She jerks her head at the next door. It is a shiny stainless steel thing with another keypad. There's also a speakeasy with a grille in the middle.

"What is the small window for?" I ask.

"Oh, I got locked inside once. That big door can only be opened from the outside—keeps anyone who goes in from getting back out with the loot."

"Then how does one leave if the door closes?"

"Just don't close the door."

Strange. She just mentioned she had the window installed to assist her in escaping should she become locked inside. There must be another way to get out. A voice-activated lock release perhaps.

We enter the brightly lit room, and my man-knickers hit the floor. "Jesus." I stand there looking at shelf after shelf of books, musical instruments, and other items, all labeled and sealed in clear plastic.

"We have autographed first editions of Austen, Twain, Tolstoy, and a bunch of others. We even have the wax mold from Elvis's first record."

"Amazing." I stroll the narrow passage, having to duck. The ceiling is low with industrial lighting every ten feet. "It is your very own Smithsonian down here."

"Well, my great-great-grandfather inherited a bunch of stuff from his great-aunt, and from there, the collection just kept growing. Someday, I'd like to open a museum. It's just that getting donors would be a full-time job."

"I think I might know a few people who would gladly contribute." Vampires are fairly big on preserving history, since we are preserved history.

I lean down and look at a large sheet of yellowed paper sealed inside a pane of glass. "Is that Shakespeare?"

There is no reply.

I look over my shoulder and do not see Miriam.

"Miriam?"

She does not reply.

"Miriam!" *Oh crap.* The door is closed. I rush to it and open the little window.

"I'm sorry, Michael." Miriam is standing just on the other side, throwing a crossbow over her shoulder. "I wasn't completely honest with you about who I am either." She turns and marches for the outer door.

What the fuck! "Miriam! Where the hell are you going with that crossbow? Come back here!"

Her reply is the thud of that outer steel door.

"Jesus Christ. I think she is a vampire hunter." Could my life possibly turn into a bigger cliché? Or an overworked storyline from the CW?

I bang my forehead against the vault's door. "Stupid. Stupid vampire." How did I fall into this trap?

Maybe because I truly do love her.

⇜ ⇝

After an hour of yelling every phrase I can think of—Abracadabra! Shazam! Fanged Love! Zorro is a sexy masked man!—through the tiny window at the alarm system, I give it a rest. I cannot believe she tricked me like this. And I'm not speaking of being locked in here. It is her secret identity that shocks me most.

But now it's all making sense—her frumpy little unassuming outfits, her Clark Kent clumsy ways, and her really smoking hot body. *And then she hides it all in those ugly tattered sweaters.*

Dammit, Vanderhorst. She pulled the bookworm wool right over my eyes. As for my attraction to her, now I'm convinced there is something more to it.

I stroll through the aisles of books and cultural

memorabilia. Most of the items are sealed inside airtight bags or encased in glass, but toward the back, on the very top shelf, is a set of twenty or so leather-bound books with dates ranging back almost three hundred years. The word *Murphy* is embossed in gold on their spines.

I pluck the first one off and start thumbing through the pages. Names, dates of birth, and family information such as the names of parents, siblings, children, and spouses are listed here. It is a very detailed family history.

"What is this?" On the last page of the chapter are notes.

Territory: Midwest

Leader: Randolph Morris

Coven Size: 64

The text goes on to describe observations about the coven—any bad apples who committed murders, notes about conversations with the leader, and the date of the kill.

What is this?

I go through several more chapters and note the same sorts of information.

I cannot believe this. I go to the last book in the series and find Miriam's parents listed. Or should I say…Miriam's mother. Mildred Murphy.

Territory: Arizona

Leader: Mr. Aspen

Size of Coven: 782

The notes go on to say that Mr. Aspen, who I replaced as leader here in Arizona, was a threat and linked to numerous murders, several forced conversions to vampirism, vampire enslavement, drug trafficking, and "other illicit activities that appear to be undermining our laws."

Our laws? Our? I scratch my chin and think. *They aren't vampire hunters. They are a vampire police of sorts?* But the "our" could signify they belong to a group of their own or…

I scan the nearby shelves. "Bingo."

The book is unmarked but sitting with the rest. I read through it, and my knees weaken. *Clive. Clive did this?* Page after page details how he formed a secret alliance with several human families, the Murphys being one, and the others are unknown to them for their own protection. The rest of the book outlines the terms of this alliance with the Murphys—their silence can never be broken, they must only kill vampires who are agreed upon by both parties as a threat, and if something should ever happen to Clive or if order among his kind is abandoned, the Murphys must hunt down and kill every last vampire. The book lists several effective defenses and ways to track us.

"I do not believe this." Clive secretly set up his own human militia. He wanted them to be prepared in case we lost the Great War.

Sneaky SOB.

I continue reading the rules of engagement. They can never disclose to a vampire what they know, who they know, or anything having to do with this alliance. And…

Each member, upon their eighteenth birthday, will be given a drop of Clive's blood. The pages say that to have his powerful blood, the blood of an original vampire, even in the minutest amount, would create a connection to him. The connection would not be detectable in their scent or alter the person in any way, but a drop of his powerful blood would cause a vampire to "*let down his or her guard*" and perhaps feel an affinity, given that original vampires are like the parents of us all.

Jesus. So that's it. There really is an attractant in Miriam's blood. *And Nice, for example, had a deep love for Clive.* They were good friends for centuries. *It would explain Nice's insatiable attraction toward Miriam. He's drawn to Clive's blood.*

As for me, I am unsure if this explains the entirety of my feelings for Miriam. Yes, Clive was my maker and I had a strong bond with him, but what exists between me and Miriam goes beyond merely feeling drawn to her. I would do anything to keep her safe and ensure she lives a long happy life. Yes, I desire her too, but my feelings are selfless not selfish.

I shake my head. *I cannot believe any of this.* Including the fact that she and her family have been helping Clive police our kind. They are an insurance policy in case anything ever happened to our own checks and balances, such as our side losing the Great War or the old guard taking over. *Just as we are seeing now.*

Once again, I am dumbfounded, yet unsurprised. It makes perfect sense. Clive believed that God made vampires for a reason: to protect this world, not prey upon the innocent.

Several hours later, I have read almost three hundred years of Murphy history. I almost feel ashamed that I have lived this long and knew Clive so well, yet I never suspected he had formed an alliance with several groups of humans.

I'll say this for Miriam; she puts on a very believable act. I do not doubt that her life was in jeopardy all the times I saved her. I do not doubt she has feelings for me. But to have the ability to pretend that you are someone else completely? A weak, mousy, clumsy librarian? *Damn, girl. You could be a vampire.* She is just that good at living a double life.

As for why she decided to lock me up down here, I do not know, and I am *furious.*

"Michael!" Footsteps thump across the floor above.

*Miriam...*I snarl to myself and place the last book back on the shelf. I get to the tiny speakeasy window just as she comes through that first door.

"Michael. Ohmygod." Miriam's face is covered in dirt and sweat, and her white blouse is torn. "You're not going to believe what I found."

I narrow my eyes. "A very angry vampire locked in a vault?"

"No. Something that actually scares me." She holds up her phone to display a photograph. "Lula."

I home in on the face in the picture. Lula is standing with a group of men surrounding her. They are all dressed in camo pants and dark shirts. She appears to be barking at them.

"Where was this taken?" I ask.

"The parking lot just outside my library. Michael, she was in on it the entire time."

"This cannot be."

Miriam closes in. "I've just spent the last two hours climbing—and perhaps falling a few times—in trees, doing nothing but taking pictures of her and some other guys coordinating thousands of men who are coming out of the ground like ants during a flood."

This is bad. Very bad. "Let me out of here," I command.

"Do you promise not to yell at me for locking you in the vault?" She smiles awkwardly.

"No."

She shrugs. "Fair enough." She looks at the alarm console on the wall. "I want to lick Mr. Darcy."

The vault door pops open.

"I knew it!" I shake a finger at her. "I knew you had some silly romance-related code phrase."

"I change it every week. Sometimes it's sci-fi or

history related."

"Awesome. Do not care." I step out of the vault. "Why did you lock me in there?" I ball my hands into tight fists. Not that I would ever harm her, but my rage needs to go somewhere, and there are too many precious items in this room.

"I'm sorry, Michael. Well…actually, no. No, I'm not." She lifts her chin. "I'm breaking every rule in the book by exposing myself to you. You did read the books, didn't you?"

"Of course. They are books and the only things not wrapped up in plastic. What sort of man would I be if I did not read them? But what sort of woman goes around parading as a librarian and killing vampires by night."

"Whoa! I have never killed anyone. And I really am a librarian."

"Then explain the frumpy clothes with a Buffy body."

"Wow." She holds up her index finger. "A, thank you for the compliment on my body. I try very hard to keep in shape." She holds up two fingers. "B, how dare you fashion-shame me. I might live in a mansion and own millions of dollars' worth of books, but that doesn't mean I'm material-istic or have money to throw away on designer clothes."

"Who said anything about designer? The clear-ance section bin at Target would be an improvement, and I know this because that's where

I buy all of my crappy teenware. If you really wanted to do your body justice, might I suggest some tiny black leather shorts?"

"Ugh! Michael, I work long hours and don't see how dressing in leather hot pants will help."

"Couldn't hurt." I shrug.

"Funny."

"Not really, because you still haven't explained why you're running off with a crossbow if you do not kill things. And by *things*, I mean vampires, which generations of your family have clearly hunted."

"I *didn't* say that I wasn't trained, because I was. My parents started when I was young. I didn't have a choice. But after I turned eighteen, they asked too much of me. Correction, they asked everything of me, and I put my foot down—a girl's gotta have time to read. I flat out rejected the whole Keepers thing."

A life without reading? I, too, would not stand for such nonsense. "Keepers. Is this what you call yourselves?"

"I honestly don't know what we're called. The different families aren't allowed to know about each other in case we get caught and tortured for info. But our family wasn't into names, so I just go with Keeper–saw it in a movie or something."

"Okay, so you rejected this, whatever you call it, and then you locked me up and ran out of here. Why?"

"I don't really have time to explain everything, but we're taught to work alone. Not that I ever worked. In fact, that was the problem. My parents wanted me to, and I thought they were crazy—all this talk about bloodsucking vampires when you've never really seen one just sounds nuts."

"And now?"

"It's still nuts, but it's all true. And you've apparently got a major *thing* for me, which is crippling your ability to think clearly. I had to lock you up so I could survey the situation. For our sake. Now we've got what we need to tackle this beast head-on. You and me."

Damn, she is making me so hot right now. Take-charge women are irresistible, even if men are better at leading. Specifically, me. The king.

"I really, really want to discuss your comment just now about my 'thing' for you," I say, "but I am far too worried about our survival." I am also gutted. If Miriam is right and that photo is showing what I think, then Lula has been working against me all along. That means she is working with Alex and our enemies. That means she helped kill Clive.

Miriam shoves her phone at me. "Take a look. I counted dozens of soldiers exiting those catacombs every few minutes for over two hours. They were being loaded onto buses."

I take her phone and flip through the images.

"Dear God. It cannot be," I mutter over a photo of Lula standing in black overalls next to Alex, Otto, and three other generals—Asia, South America, and Canada.

Those sneaky Canadian bastards. Always appearing so neutral and friendly. Going forward, I shall know better; however, what shocks me most is the man facing them. He has shaggy dark brown hair and a medium build. His face is so familiar, I could draw every wrinkle, every feature from memory.

"Clive." I feel like the wind's been knocked out of me. "He's not dead?" I do not know how to process this. There is a vacuum where emotion should reside. *He's alive.* The man—who was the only father I ever knew, who allowed me to mourn him and suffer the rage of believing he was murdered—has been alive the entire time.

My mind begins sliding the pieces of my mystery into place: Who could pull the right strings to have me appointed king when there were better candidates? Who could convince my good friend Alex to betray everyone, including me? Who would be able to turn Lula against me?

Clive. Clive. Clive. Only someone like him, a first-generation vampire and legend to our people, has that much power.

I suddenly realize why Clive did all those favors for so many vampires. He ran his detective agency into the ground, but in the meantime he was firming up loyalty and planning all this.

As for my new appointment, Clive must have wanted someone in charge whom he could easily manipulate, and that person would be me. He knows exactly what makes me tick. He knows my every weakness and strength. This is how he managed to distract me while he worked quietly behind the scenes. In short, I have been unknowingly supporting Clive this entire time. *I am the king who cannot take action because he's too busy chasing red herrings and protecting a librarian.* Essentially making our side a snake with a useless head.

I cannot believe that all along it was Clive, but the pieces fit. *Except one: Why?* Clive fought for hundreds of years to bring our race to heel. Why destroy his legacy?

"I need to sit down," I say. "Got any chocolate? Or cookies with chocolate? Really, anything with chocolate will do."

"You're hungry? Now?" Miriam asks.

"Chocolate is a narcotic for my kind, and I'm in need of sedation." How does she not know this? *Grandpa Kipper knew.*

"Yeah...no. You need to be lucid because we have to do something, and I don't think baking cookies is going to cut it."

"Then clearly you understand nothing about war," I grumble.

"Michael, stop it! This is serious."

"Really? Because this feels like one giant clown orgy to me." I scrub my face with my hands.

"I understand you're upset. I do. But now that we know where these bad vampires are, who's leading, and what they are up to, we have enough to make a move."

"And which move might that be? Lighting our hair on fire and running away screaming?" Honestly, it sounds kind of pleasant, because if I'm facing having to go up against Clive, Lula, Alex, Otto, and several other generals, I might as well Ginsu my genitals and hand them over.

"We need to warn everyone," Miriam says.

"What good will that do? The enemy has their claws in everything. A warning would simply be used by them to create countermeasures."

"Who cares! Do the math, Michael. Your fifteen thousand two hundred and fifty-seven vampires compared to their what? Two thousand? All you need to do is warn everyone. If a society is attacked, tell them to send out an alert. Order the surrounding territories to send in help."

"You know our exact population?"

"Don't you?"

Nope. "I guess I forgot." But it is a bit frightening how much these Keepers know. And here I thought we were being sly vampires on the down low.

"Let's get the hell out of here while we still can," Miriam says. "We'll send an email from the road."

"Where's Viviana?" I ask. She was not in those photos.

"Oh, I think she was tied up in your office."

Dammit. "We have to help her."

"Michael," Miriam grabs my arm, "I am a complete idiot when it comes to warfare, but I'll tell you this: you're way too nice. She is bait."

"How do you know this?"

"Because I have a brain."

I start to mull. Viviana claims to have been turned against her will and forced to work for Jeremy and his boss, but I never verified her story before deciding to keep her on. She could have made the whole thing up. *And she did help organize the blood auctions.* Plus, she makes sure my coffee is perfect every morning and does it with a smile.

"She's a mole, isn't she?" I say, thinking about all the little red herrings she's been throwing out. *"We can't get any guards." "Oh, let's check the RSVPs to the ball."* She was helping to distract me all along, keeping me off Clive's trail. She even made sure I'd think Clive was dead by giving me his ashes.

"Yes." Miriam nods. "One hundred percent yes."

I will never trust anyone again. "Is the cabin you spoke of still safe?"

Thump! Thump! Thump! Multiple footsteps storm across the floor above.

"They're here." Miriam removes her crossbow from her back and grips it firmly.

"Have you ever used that thing?" I ask.

"God no. But I'm a librarian; if we want to learn how to do something, we read a book."

"And you've read one about the use of crossbows?" I find it interesting that such a book exists.

"Yes. Stop it! We have to go. There's an exit through there." She points to the vault. "I parked your car right outside."

"This isn't another trick, is it?" I ask.

"No. There's a doorway hidden behind those shelves you were perusing."

"Dammit, woman. Why are you so smart?"

"I already told you, Michael. I'm a librarian."

"And a very sexy one." I am extremely turned on by this gung ho, crossbow-carrying, fearless side of her. "I cannot wait to make love to you again."

"Seriously? You're thinking of sex right now?"

"I am a vampire. That is what we do when we get excited."

"Touché."

We run into the vault, securing the door behind us, and escape in my blue shoebox. I cannot believe how this day unfolded. Clive, my maker, is still alive. He is the evil force behind everything and has been manipulating me from day one. My best friend, Lula, has stabbed me right in the heart, presenting me with lie after lie. Our best generals are in on this coup along with God only knows how many soldiers. Without a doubt, the world is about to fall on dark times. Yet, somehow, I feel a sense of relief. Miriam, too, has been putting on her own charade. She is not the timid or weak woman I believed her to be. She carries a crossbow.

She just might be the most perfect woman I have ever met.

CHAPTER FOURTEEN

Miriam and I hit the road. I have just enough battery charge in my stupid car to get us to her cabin by taking the backroads versus the freeway. We both agreed that while the freeway would be faster, there is a greater chance of being spotted by Clive's soldiers, who—as Miriam witnessed—are being loaded into buses. I can only assume they're being deployed to their targets. That is why Clive wanted me out of his hair and following a dead lead in Blackpool. This entire time, their army was right below our noses somewhere in the miles of catacombs below the city.

Now that army is on the move, and I'm guessing it is to California. I mean, honestly, if you're going to take over any state, California is a great choice. *So many crazies.* It is as if they make them en masse and pump them out of a factory. *Especially that San Francisco.*

My second guess is that they are going to hit the Las Vegas territory—the Society of the Lucky Lady—whose human front promotes responsible gambling, but is really the HQ for Nevada, the rest of the West Coast, and Utah together. My territory, which includes New Mexico, is already dead in the water since the de facto leader, Lula, is in on everything and there are no guards or military force to be heard of. I'm sure whoever Otto was sending my way on charade night were men loyal to him. So, in short, with a few strategic attacks, Clive will take the West in a day. The Midwest will be an easy target, as the vampire populations are very scattered, and it seems our second global headquarters in Wellington, Kansas, is already in on this whole thing, since that post has been abandoned. Ohio belonged to Clive before I took over, and most of the families were loyal to him—or will be once he asks them to follow him. Even if they disagree with his agenda, they will not want to cross such a man. Vampires follow power, not titles.

The southern territories, which includes Texas, will be a toss-up. The states of that region are notorious for trusting no one and will fight tooth and nail against any outsiders. Canada is already lost since their general is part of Team Human Enslavement. I suspect Clive already has parts of Mexico in his pocket since they've been building relationships with the cartel. *Another piece of the puzzle solved.* Somehow, the cartel got involved with this whole blood-trafficking thing. I believed it to be about money, and possibly it was, but there was more to it. Clive probably promised to take out one group's rivals in exchange for support when the time came.

The East Coast will be a battleground for certain. In fact, if I had an army, I would be sending every able body there to prepare.

But you do not have an army. Nevertheless, this doesn't mean those territories wouldn't want to fight.

"Miriam, are you almost done with the email and text?" I glance at her typing away on my phone from the passenger seat. The early morning sun is beaming through the window, the rays of light catching the golden hues in her blonde hair. She looks tired, dirty from her tree hopping, and more gorgeous than ever. Could it be because I am seeing this new side of her?

"Yeah. I think so," she replies.

"We need to tell everyone in the US to evacuate to the East Coast if they are not already there."

"Huh?" Miriam blinks at me, looking up from the phone.

"Clive and his generals have the same information we do. They know they can easily take every territory except for certain pockets in the South and the entire East Coast. If I send a warning out to everyone to move quickly—get in their cars, get on planes, do whatever they must to head east to fight—it won't matter if our enemies find out. In fact, I would argue that it will help us. Clive will know that he's lost the element of surprise. He will know that we are not going to put up a fight in any other territories, so they might actually back off the West and Midwest. No deaths. No fighting."

"I see your point. If there's no one to fight, they'll have to regroup and prepare for a different battle."

"Yes. And we will be ready. If we can defeat them on the East Coast, then they're done. They will not have enough men to take South America, Europe, or anywhere else."

"Plus, think of all the lives saved if you make Clive and his army come directly to you. One battle. Winner takes all."

"Well, they would get the East Coast, but frankly, that's not the end of the world. Do you know how cold it gets in New York in the winter? It's troubling. But if we can stop them there, we've won."

Miriam nods. "I like it. I'll modify the messages." She taps in a bunch of letters on my phone and reads the note back to me. It's brief, but to the point, informing everyone that Clive is alive and well and is coordinating an attack on our way of life for reasons unknown to us. It lists all of the generals who are participating in this act of treason and instructs everyone to evacuate immediately to the territories in the east to prepare for battle.

"Make sure that you add 'by order of the king' to that last part so they know it is not optional," I say.

"Got it."

We include a few more notes for the rest of the world to send reinforcements, too, but to leave themselves well guarded. *Hold until further instructions.*

"All right," says Miriam, "here we go." She hits send on the email. "Oh no."

"What?"

"I don't have a signal." She lifts the phone closer to the window.

"Try sending it as a text." We'd planned to do both anyway. Some vampires really hate email.

"Same thing."

"I am certain the signal will strengthen up ahead." At the moment, we are in the middle of the desert with nothing but Joshua trees, saguaro cacti, rocks, and lizards.

"Michael?"

"Yes?"

"I really have to pee."

"Now?" I snap.

"I'm sorry. I've been holding it for over an hour."

I glance in the rearview mirror. There is no one behind us, and we've only passed a few cars. It appears to be safe, but one never knows. "Just make it fast."

"Personally, I like to pee slowly when my bladder is about to explode. Prolongs the suffering," she says sarcastically.

"Haha." Up ahead I spot a small rocky hill with some thorny bushes about, so I pull off. "Just watch for rattlesnakes."

Miriam looks at me.

I look at her.

"Aren't you coming with me?" she says.

"No. Better I remain here and—"

Beep! Beep! Beep! The ear-piercing sound comes from both our phones. *Beep! Beep! Beep!*

"Well," says Miriam, "the good news is we just got reception and the email went out. The bad news is there's a haboob warning in effect that went out twenty minutes ago."

"Of course there is," I say dryly, noting how when life goes to hell in a handbasket, it typically comes with a side of "Oh-come on!" and "What-theshit."

"Yep. There it is." Miriam hangs her head out the window. "And it looks like a really bad one."

Haboob is a fancy term for a giant horrible dust storm preceding a monsoon rain. The storm front is so powerful that as it pushes through, it picks up dirt from the desert floor. Meaning, we are about to be engulfed in a thick cloud of windy dry grit, followed by enough rain to fill the Colorado River in two minutes. It is really fun. If you enjoy being dirty and soggy.

"Hurry, then. We only have a few minutes," I tell Miriam.

She gives me a look.

"Fine. I will go with you." I throw my hands in the air.

"Thanks."

We exit the car, me following closely behind, watching her do a mixture of a pee-pee dance and a speed walk. If we were not in such a dire situation, I would laugh. As is, however, I settle for a fat smirk.

Miriam ducks behind a bolder, and I turn my back.

"Oh, sounds like the monsoon rain is here," I joke.

"I told you I had to go."

"I find it interesting how our relationship has already progressed to this level so quickly. Normally, one waits until the third or fourth round of coitus before they share such delight—"

"Ow! Son of a!" Miriam squawks.

I turn to see Miriam pulling up her jeans, hopping on one foot.

"Are you all right? Did something bite you?" I try not to panic.

"Yes! Ow!"

I scoop her up into my arms and swivel, looking for the offender. *Please do not let it be a snake. Please do not let it be a...*

I notice a line of tiny red ants marching around the yellow puddle she's left behind.

"You peed on their house and made them unhappy." I jerk my head and stare down at the spot. "They will not be sending you a birthday card, but you will survive."

I set her down, away from the angry wet ants.

"Man, that hurts." She rubs her ankle. "It's like

my skin is on fire."

"Come on, we need to go. Perhaps we can stop at a convenience store up ahead and find some ice." Either way, the violent weather is about to hit us, and it will not be safe for driving.

I take her warm little hand, and we head back to the car. Miriam freezes and jerks free from my grip.

"Michael? Where is the *caca azul?*" Her eyes lock on the road, and I turn my head.

"I-I—" My mouth flaps for a moment while my mind tries to understand how our vehicle has disappeared.

"Please don't tell me you left the key inside."

I glance north and then south, down the length of the road. "But we were only... I just looked away for a... Hell, I can't believe this." I lean my head back and look up at the sky. The sun is fading as the particulate matter increases. "All right. We will simply flag down the next car."

"I don't know, Michael. Hitchhiking isn't safe."

"For them or for us? Because I am a vampire, so I am fairly sure I am the one their mothers warned them about."

"Good point."

"Ah. Here comes someone now." It is a large white van driving like a bat out of hell.

I raise my arm, attempting to flag it down, but they pass right on by. "Well, that didn't go so—"

The van screeches to a halt, smoke spewing from the friction on the asphalt.

I notice the heads of several tall men through the back windows. *Uh-oh.* "Run, Miriam."

"Huh?"

"Run! Those men are not stopping to give us a ride. They are soldiers. Vampire soldiers." I count five, which I can easily take out, except one goes straight after Miriam, and four rush at me.

Dammit. Dammit! The first one—a tall man with short dark hair, wearing camo pants and a black T-shirt like the rest—is done for with a snap of the neck. He didn't even see it coming. I am faster, stronger, and did I mention that I earned the name "the Executioner" for a damned good reason?

The second man comes at me, and we're trapped in a cloud of dust. No, not the haboob. His friend's remains. Of course, I am used to fighting in such conditions, so the second man is down and blowing with the wind before men three and four even know what's happened.

I am ready to run after Miriam as soon as I execute these two clowns, but a scream shuts me down.

Miriam. I glance over my shoulder. One man has her by the throat and lifted into the air, her feet kicking wildly.

"If you harm her," I warn, "you will have nothing left to bargain with, and I will not be offering a pleasant dusting for any of you."

The man stares me down with his dark eyes while Miriam claws at his hands, gasping for air.

"Put. Her. Down," I growl.

"Get in the van, and we will think about letting her live."

Just then the dust storm hits us. Sand whips through our hair and clothes.

"Okay." I raise my hands, squinting. "Just put her down, and I will come quietly."

The man sets her on the dirt but doesn't release his grip. "One false move, and I'll crush her wind-pipe."

I nod, keeping my hands up.

The man starts walking Miriam toward the van while the other two stay behind me and offer assistance with a little shove.

"Move it, your majesty," one says with a snicker.

"You know, it's too late," I say. "We've already alerted all five hundred and eighty-two societies. Those who are not with you will be gathering quickly to end you."

"No. They won't," the guy responds. "Because you're going to tell everyone to stand down."

"What makes you think I would do that?" I ask.

"Because we'll kill your librarian if you don't."

Like I said before, Miriam is my biggest weakness. This is exactly what I feared.

"Jesus!" one man yells from behind me, and I hear a screech.

I turn just in time to see my little car plowing into the two men behind me. I jump out of the way. Both men evaporate into a cloud of gray dust that mixes with the brown haze circulating about us.

I don't know what is happening or who is behind the wheel, but this is my chance.

I rush to Miriam, taking advantage of my speed, and shove my hand straight through her captor's chest. I yank out his heart and he turns to dust, leaving Miriam standing there covered head to toe in light gray powder.

"Vanderhorsthssth!"

Miriam and I both turn our heads to see Mr. Nice hopping from my car.

"Oh hell." I put myself between her and him. "What are you doing here?"

"I have been following you. So have they." He leans sideways to peer around me. "Are you all right, my sweet, sweet love-dumpling?"

"You stole our car?" I ask.

"Yesss…how else was I to lure them away? On foot?"

"So, you've been running behind us the entire time?"

"Of course, silly. Then I saw zi empty car, and instead of warning you, I decided to hop in and lure them away for a Nice ambush up ahead. But they did not come, and that is because you mucked it up. Didn't anyone ever tell you that hitchhiking is unsafe, Vanderhorsthssst? Bad vampire!"

"Thank you. I guess?" I'm unsure what he intends to do now.

"Well, there are more coming, so *choo* best be on your *ways* now," Nice says. "I will hold them off while you make your escape."

It amazes me how his accent is so unpredictable.

He's like grammatical roulette. You just never know what you are going to get.

"How many more?" I ask.

"Twelve or so. I will play zi pattycake with their arms for a little while. You may go now."

The image of Nice tearing off their limbs and beating these men to death pops into my head. I almost want to stay and watch simply because his torture skills are legendary.

"Off with you!" He looks straight at Miriam. "And do not forget, my little book-dove, what the Nice has done for you today. All for your sweet, sweet love."

"You want my first edition of *Pride and Prejudice*, don't you?"

Nice went to her house once and flipped out when he saw her collection, that book in particular. "A token of your love for me, my little paper worshiper."

"It's yours," she says. "But as a token of gratitude and nothing more."

Nice shrugs. "Hold all judgment until you have seen my book collection. You will change your tune." He chuckles sadistically.

"Let's go." I grab Miriam's hand and lead her to the car. We get in and zoom away just as the rain starts to come down in buckets. It is far too dangerous to drive, but I must.

"Wow. When it rains, it pours," Miriam mutters.

"Let us hope this is the last storm for the day."

CHAPTER FIFTEEN

After a brief pause at a rest stop, where Miriam throws up and then grills me about vampire-human procreation, we are back on the road.

"So you're sure I'm not pregnant, right?"

This is such a bizarre conversation to be having at the moment. I have been betrayed by everyone I ever trusted, sent on a wild-goose chase to Blackpool, cornered by soldiers, and then saved by Mr. Nice, who was running on foot behind us for over sixty miles. Now we are talking about pregnancy?

"I am certain you are not. You are reacting to extreme stress. It is perfectly normal. Also, we only had sex a day ago. No one gets pregnant that fast."

"Bella did," Miriam mutters and then sips on her bottled water, which I procured from the rest-stop vending machine.

"Come again?" I say.

"Never mind." Miriam looks out the window. Her face is pale and her heartbeat still elevated.

"You must breathe. Try to calm yourself so the adrenaline can leave your body."

"How can I? The world as we know it is about to end—I mean, once people find out about you, they're going to go apeshit. I'm literally witnessing the end of an era where humans think they are at the top of the food chain. Worst of all, I had to leave my books—now more important than ever because they are a record of life before all this—and you can't even look at me."

"Not true. I am looking at you now." I flash a glance her way. "All right, I am looking at the road because it is getting quite curvy since we have reached the mountains, but I have looked at you plenty."

"I'm not stupid, Michael. And you promised to be honest with me."

"What, pray tell, woman, do you think I'm hiding?"

"Ever since I told you about my grandpa Kipper and my parents being Keepers, you haven't looked at me the same. By the way, everything I told you was a test. It was true, but I said it so I could see how you'd react—how certain you are about us."

I nod, understanding her position. "And I failed."

"Yes."

I whoosh out a breath. "I admit that I fear—or feared—there were forces beyond my control inducing my emotions."

"Why?" she snaps. "Because it would be so damned impossible for the great Michael Vanderhorst to want a simple little librarian who constantly trips on her shoelaces?"

"No. Not at all. I find your lack of coordination quite charming. My doubt comes from the fact it is impossible that such a magnificent, shockingly beautiful and intelligent woman would want a man like me. I am over four centuries old. My baggage is only outnumbered by my number of kills."

"Michael." She lays her hand on my thigh. "I think you are unlike any man I've ever met. Human or otherwise. You're loyal and compassionate, and if that's the result of you killing thousands of blood-thirsty, murdering vampires or horrible people who do nothing but hurt others, then you'll hear zero complaints from me. My only question for you, Michael Vanderhorst, is whether you're protecting me out of a sense of obligation or because you really love me."

Such a loaded question, but I am no different than her in this moment. I need answers. I think about everything we've been through since we met a little over a month ago. There was this initial attraction that dumbfounded me, followed by the need to protect her at all costs. I could only think of being near her, even if she was in mourning, still in love with her boyfriend and completely unable to reciprocate my affection. In short, what I felt and still feel is unconditional.

I even stayed in Phoenix, forgoing all creature comforts, simply to work for minimum wage as her part-time assistant. *Eeesh...that studio.* Roaches, grime, and other unidentifiable substances caked in every corner. I could have gone home after the case surrounding Clive's death had been closed—even if false. Then, after being appointed the leader of the Arizona Society of Sunshine Disappointment, as well as the Cincinnati Historical Society of Original Family Members, I could have ditched the gig with Miriam and changed my cover story to allow for a more lavish lifestyle, yet I did not. I wanted to continue working for her, staying by her side even when I lost hope that she could desire anything from me besides my excellent book reshelving skills. *All along I was in it for her company.*

I clear my throat, knowing Miriam is waiting for an answer: Do I truly love her, or is my attraction a side effect of some supernatural force at work, the result of her having ingested a drop of Clive's blood as described in those Keeper books? Perhaps. But would that explain what I feel in my heart or how she's woken up my soul from a long deep slumber?

I pull off in a turnout so she can look into my eyes when I say this. "Miriam, none of what you've told me explains how—after four hundred years of existence, when I have never loved anyone or anything—I have these feelings for you." I blink. "And your first editions. So while I cannot tell you with one hundred percent certainty what drew me into your library that morning, I can tell you that I trust what is in my heart. I feel nothing but love for you."

Miriam looks at me for a long awkward moment. "I'm not giving you a raise, if that's what you're after."

"I'll take sex and some occasional naked spooning as payment."

"Deal." She slides her warm, soft hand to the nape of my neck and pulls me in for a kiss that starts off as simple but quickly evolves into something more. Groping, panting, and lapping.

I want to take her right here, right now, but it is daylight, and we need to get out of sight.

I pull away. "We must go. But I assure you I will not be using my hands to steer the remainder of the way."

She glances at my manhood and the prominent tent in my jeans. "I can't believe how talented you are with that thing."

I nod. "Let us finish the journey, and I promise to bang you and fang you to your heart's content." Her words, not mine.

"Just as long as you remember that this is supposed to be a PG13 mystery," she says.

"I had intended it to be family friendly, so the upgrade is a relief, because my thoughts for you are very R-rated."

"Thank God. Because mine are XX. Maybe even XXX."

"Are you saying that your feelings are purely carnal?" I ask.

"Do you think I would break every rule in the

book if that were true? Keepers do not expose themselves to vampires. And forget about sleeping with one." She blinks and adds, "Who looks to be ten years younger, therefore making her a giant perv only after arm candy."

"I am having trouble deciphering your remarks," I say. "Are you happy? Do you trust that I love you and will do everything within my power to keep you safe?"

"Without a doubt."

"That is all I need to know, then." Our mouths collide, and I go into a frenzied state of male need. The need to lick her from head to toe. The need to kiss her until my heart stops. The need to be inside her and make her climax until she can take no more.

I pull out onto the freeway, hitting the accelerator.

"Someone's in a hurry," she says.

"I've waited my entire life for you, and I am all out of patience."

CHAPTER SIXTEEN

Miriam and I travel down a long dirt road before finally arriving to the small A-frame cabin about ten miles north of Flagstaff. The pine-scented morning air is cool and crisp—lovely—but the property is not fenced in, and the dense forest around us is strategically undesirable. The trees could provide cover for anyone wishing to attack.

Not that they will find us. Nevertheless, we cannot stay here long. A day or two at the most. Then we must make our way east like everyone else.

Miriam finds her key under a rock and then pops open the door. The musty smell of dust pours outside onto the wooden porch, which is covered in dirt, pinecones, and leaves.

"When's the last time you were here?" I ask while she deactivates the alarm.

"A few years. Really, not since my parents died."

"Did you come here often with them?" I wonder.

"When I was little. Like I said, my mother used this cabin the most—her little getaway. I would come every once in a while for snowboarding."

"You snowboard?"

She shrugs, closes the door, and then goes to the fuse box in the corner. "Yes, Michael. Me and my two left feet are actually pretty good."

Interesting.

"Do you ski or do any sports?" she asks.

"My outdoor activities are generally limited to digging holes to hide bodies."

She hits a couple of switches, and I hear the open refrigerator kick on. "If they had an Olympic sport of body disposal, you would win."

"I would, wouldn't I?" I realize we are both just making small talk. What's really on our minds is something else.

"Do you want to take a bath or have a shower? Are you hungry?" She walks over to the small kitchenette in the corner. It's basic with white appliances. The flooring is made of pine planks, but the stairs, leading up to what I assume are several bedrooms, are carpeted.

"Are you proposing to feed me?" I ask. "Because I already told you, I do not think it is safe. You are much too delicious."

She reaches for a drawer under the counter and produces a menu. "Chinese takeout. We can ask them to make it extra spicy."

I really could go for some fiery eggplant, but… "We'd better stay put. Besides, I am still digesting a serial killer from a few days ago. Are you *hungry*?" I ask.

She bobs her head. "I could go for a snack." She

eyes the length of my body.

I'm suddenly too aroused to continue with our awkward little chat.

I pull off my shirt and kick off my shoes. I then get to unbuttoning my pants. She watches intently as I shed my clothes right there in the living room.

"You are an impressive sight." Her heartbeat accelerates, and the scent of her flushed skin fills the room.

"I boxed and played a lot of rugby in my youth. I was lucky enough to be turned while I was in excellent shape, though I might have appreciated looking just a bit older."

She smiles. "You must get tired of being card-ed."

I tilt my head. "I am standing naked in your living room. Would you like to continue the small talk or be taken upstairs for a solid pounding?"

She blinks. "First door on the left."

I flash a devilish smile before swooping in, throwing her over my shoulder, and taking her upstairs. The bed has linens, but I'm sure they are dusty, so I peel back the blanket and toss it to the floor.

I set her down on her back and lay myself over her. When our mouths meet, the taste of her on my tongue instantly sets me off. I kiss her hard, trying to avoid any accidents with my fangs even if I want a nibble. She is far too tempting.

I pull off her tattered white shirt and savor the

feel of her warm skin against me. This woman heats me up, inside and out.

I work off her pants and get her completely naked, never leaving her mouth and those wild kisses for more than a moment.

She moves against me, touching my arms, my hips, my ass. I know I should go slow, but it is impossible. She drives me insane with desire. *How could I ever doubt what we have?*

I settle between her thighs and move myself into position, trailing kisses down her neck. I know she wants this. I know I must be careful.

I bite down and thrust inside her. Both are like heaven, and her sharp moans tell me she is right there with me. Like before, I only go deep where she needs it. Her neck, on the other hand, is just a nick for her pleasure and mine.

"Kiss me," she pants, our bodies moving together with urgency.

The fact that she wants to taste herself on my tongue sets me off. I'm ready but must wait.

Our mouths lock and our tongues lash in time to the movements of me inside her. Her every whimper only makes it harder for me to control myself. I want the release. I need the release, but it must be perfect.

I listen to her breaths and heartbeat. I smell the sweet scent of her arousal in the air, infused into her fresh sweat. She is ready.

I quicken the pace and go deeper, letting what

nature gave me do its job. She responds by lifting her hips and digging her nails into my back.

This is it. She wants it hard. She wants me to give her what she needs.

I slam into her one last time, and she throws her head back. I let go and fill her with everything I can give. Her climax only increases the pleasure of my release, every twitch of her body around my shaft prolonging the moment.

I am completely lost to her. This thing between us is powerful, and a part of me realizes just how dangerous that is because there is nothing I wouldn't do for her.

I return my mouth to hers and plant a lingering kiss on her lips. She tastes even sweeter now. Maybe because she is sated and, for the moment, not thinking about the last few days. Perhaps it is because she is in love.

I roll off her so she can catch her breath.

"Wow," she pants. "There are no words."

"Did your ex ever…" My voice fades.

She stares up at the ceiling. "Did he what?"

"Perhaps the question is too indelicate," I say.

"Jeremy and I never had sex, if that's what you're asking."

"You didn't?" I roll to my side and prop my head up with an elbow and an arm.

"No. I mean, he tried to persuade me, but I used the excuse of my parents and still being in mourning—which I was—to keep him away. I told him he traveled a lot, and I wouldn't sleep with him until he was ready to settle down and make a commitment."

"So you never loved him," I conclude.

"No. I knew what he was the entire time."

"You did?" I find this shocking. "Why did you pretend to be surprised when I told you he was a vampire?"

"All part of my training. If I didn't act surprised, you would wonder why and become suspicious. I'm supposed to be a normal, regular person, and normal people don't believe vampires exist. They think you're insane if you try to convince them otherwise."

Ah. Thus the reason she had a hissy when I attempted to tell her what I was.

She goes on, "I just couldn't figure out what Jeremy was up to. Then I started getting threatening calls about selling my property. Strange men began coming to my home. I kept thinking that this Clive person would show up and tell me what to do—I mean, he seemed to be running the whole Keeper deal. I certainly didn't want to get involved, but at the same time, I felt obligated to learn what I could, so I played along and kept to my script."

"Wow. Just…wow." I shake my head in awe of her. "And I think I am good at running with a cover story. You had me completely convinced."

"My parents trained me well."

"Did you know I was a vampire?" I ask.

"When we first met, no. But then you showed up at the hospital, and I miraculously healed." Those "land developers" wouldn't give up trying to get her land and sent thugs after her several times. One man nearly broke her skull, and I had no choice but to sneak her some of my blood to heal her.

She adds, "I barely knew you, but you saved me. It contradicted so much about what I was taught."

"Which is?"

"You're all cold-hearted killers. Just that some of you keep yourselves in line and some don't. The whole point of the Keepers was ensuring humans could defeat you 'vicious vampires' if the Great War didn't go our way. I think, though, after victory was declared, Clive knew there would always be bad vampires. He didn't trust your laws and councils, and he felt obligated to make sure we weren't lambs for the slaughter—as you put it."

I sigh with frustration. Clive worked tirelessly to win the Great War and ensure humans would be safe from us. *So why is he now trying to undo it?* It just doesn't make any sense.

Mystery! Mystery! Mystery!

Stop it. There will be no more rejoicing over unanswered questions.

"One thing is certain," I say, "Clive is very old and very cunning. He does not think like we do."

"How so?" Miriam asks.

"He is a meticulous planner and extremely patient—a result of being immortal and having lived so long. But he is a master at strategizing. I believe this is why he pulled strings to put me in place as king and then distracted me with misinformation. Someone had to lead, and he wanted a person who would be predictable and whom he could easily control." For example, the entire time I was in transit between Phoenix and Blackpool, Clive's generals and men were all coming to Phoenix to prepare for their attack. Clive had been able to get me completely out of the way, on a plane, running around looking for the council members in the UK. I suspect it is the same reason he made sure I was appointed leader of the Arizona Society of Sunshine Masochists. He would rather it be me leading Arizona and Cincinnati, which I inherited upon his "death," because he knew exactly how to handle me. He didn't want a stranger, a wildcard, messing up his plans. With Lula and Viviana in on everything, he had me under complete control.

"So what are we going to do next?" Miriam asks. "Because if what you say is true, then he will have a contingency for everything."

"Everything except the irrational," I mutter. "Which is why I must be unpredictable."

"How do you propose to do that?"

I am suddenly on top of her, pinning her wrists. "By doing things like this." I kiss her neck and blow little raspberries.

"Stop it!" She laughs and squirms. "I hate being

tickled. And I need to pee."

"You're no fun. All these bio breaks make me think I should turn you into a vampire."

"No, thank you. I meant what I said about my mortality. Life only has meaning because its supply is limited. Just like gold."

I roll off her and she scurries out into the hallway and into the bathroom. Meanwhile, I think about what she just said. I was joking about her becoming a vampire, of course, but a part of me wants to give her all the "gold" in the world. I cannot stand the thought of her growing old and dying. Our relationship is doomed, yet I cannot let her go. I see that now.

"Hey." Miriam stands in the doorway wearing a robe. "I'm getting some water and a snack. Want anything?"

"Yes, but it requires a partner, so hurry back."

"Sounds fun." She marches downstairs, and my mind drifts. For over a month, Miriam was pretending, and so was I. It is a miracle we ended up falling in love despite not showing our true selves until now.

But what an actress. Almost the entire time she knew I was a vampire. It explains why she suddenly did not seem too hung up on the news when we got on that plane. After I snatched her from my apartment at light speed, she realized she couldn't carry on with her own charade—i.e., telling me vampires weren't real, the reaction of a "normal" person.

However, even then, she proceeded with caution and kept to her script.

I am glad she finally decided to trust me, because now I see the real woman who's been hiding behind those intelligent eyes, and she is amazing.

"Michael! Come down here. You need to check this out!"

I rush downstairs in the buff, thinking my worst nightmare has just come true and we're surrounded.

"Look!" She holds up my phone.

"God. You scared me." I take the device and begin scrolling. Hundreds of texts are coming in, most of them saying the same thing: they will see me on the East Coast and fight anyone who threatens our peaceful way of life. A few say they'd rather die than give up a world with Quesaritos and *Fortnite.* "*No way am I going back to* The Flintstones.*"* Most simply say they are furious and on their way. Messages from all over the world indicate reinforcements are already in the air.

With so many on our side and moving quickly into place, it will be difficult for our enemies to take us out.

"You did it, Michael. I'm sure Clive and his army weren't expecting everyone to pull together like this."

My phone rings and the caller ID is blocked. "Hello?"

"Hello, Michael."

I feel the floor of my stomach fall out like a

trapdoor that's been sprung. It is a voice that, up until today, I never thought I would hear again. I am furious. "Clive."

"I hear you've been busy."

"Not as busy as you, Clive." I feel strange having this conversation in the buff, so I pick up my jeans off the floor where I left them and slide them on, holding the phone with my shoulder.

"Yes, well, I have my reasons, and you're getting in the way."

"Good. Because someone has to stop you," I reply.

"Why would you want to do that?" His voice is calm and smug, not at all like the caring but firm man I used to know.

"You are *not* going to undo all of our hard work. Too many sacrifices were made, too many lives lost just to get where we are. I won't let anyone throw that away because you have lost your shit."

"You are upset with me, Michael. And rightly so. I allowed you to think I was dead. I used you as a pawn, but ask yourself why I would go through all this trouble if my reasons weren't just."

"I *have* asked myself. Repeatedly. The blood farm, the murders, the treason against our societies. None of it is excusable."

"Really? Because look around you, Michael. Look at what is happening. We gave control to humans over three hundred years ago. Since then, they've polluted the air, killed off thousands of species, and filled the oceans with toxic waste and plastic. This planet is dying."

This is why he wants to overthrow our government? "So your plan is to kill off everyone who believed in your dream and followed you, doing things they are not proud of, all to enslave humans and save the planet?"

"I plan to restore the natural order. There is no other way, Michael. If we do not, we all die."

He sounds like a poster child for Green Peace, but with an added sprinkle of mass murder and apocalyptic war. "I am sorry, Clive, but think about what you are saying; you want a world where people are kept in cages, made to serve us and be our food. It's barbaric, and even if I agreed with you, there are far more of them than there are of us."

"We didn't get to the place we are in overnight. The same goes for undoing it. We will make things right, but we must all stick together."

"Millions of people and thousands of vampires will die in the process."

"We are dead anyway if we do nothing," he replies.

"There is a better way. We can stay in the shadows. We can persuade and influence from positions of power."

"It will take too long. Humans had their chance. They failed. End of story. All you need to decide is if you and your librarian would like to join us, or make this your last day on earth."

I hear a crunch outside through the closed door, a twig snapping fifty yards away. *Crap.* "You're here."

"Thought I taught you better, Michael," says Clive. "Always check under your car for tracking devices."

Dammit. I screwed up. That's why my car was left parked at the airport. Clive knew I would be too preoccupied protecting Miriam to remember to check.

I look at Miriam, who has been standing there staring with bated breath the entire time.

I cannot live in a world where she is treated like cattle or isn't free to live her life, hoarding her books. So if I have to choose between a world that is going to hell in a handbasket with a side order of whattheshit, or a world where humans—the species we are born into—are treated like animals, I take the handbasket. I simply do not see the point in living if to do so means losing everything decent and good inside me. I have given up too much to become a monster.

"See you outside." I end the call.

"Well? What happened?" Miriam asked.

I hang my head. "We are surrounded. I am fairly sure Clive is outside as well."

Miriam covers her mouth and gasps. "Oh no."

"The good news is, I have my answers—Clive believes the Great War was a mistake and now plans to put humans in cages. He says it is the only way to save the planet and ourselves. The bad news I can either join him or die, and I'm fairly sure you'll die regardless of what I do."

Miriam's face turns pale. "There has to be something we can do."

I nod. "There is. I can fight."

"You mean alone? Out there?"

I nod.

"But Clive is a first-generation vampire. He's stronger than you."

"I have little other choice. If I go along with him, they'll take you and kill you, likely to test my loyalty. If I fight and lose, they will kill you. My only chance is to fight and win."

Miriam goes over to the couch and sinks down. "Oh my God." She scrubs her face with her hands. "This doesn't make any sense. Clive trained the Keepers. He put measures in place to prevent a takeover like this."

"Clearly he changed his mind, Miriam. And I wouldn't doubt for a moment that your parents' death was planned. He probably only let you live because you refused to be a part of the program."

She lifts her head, and her eyes fill with tears. "You really think that?"

Clive used to always tell me that being a detective was more like solving math problems than anything else. Take a question, plug in an answer, and see if it fits. From day one, Clive had planned everything—faking his death, aligning himself with the Mexican drug cartel, decades of buying loyalty by doing free work, the blood farm, putting me in charge and using his knowledge of my weaknesses to manipulate me. How could I put it past him to murder Miriam's parents? The answer is, I can't. "It looked like an accident, but the timing was too perfect. He couldn't risk your parents finding out what he was up to and getting in the way. I'm sure he killed all of the Keepers. It's what I would do if I were an evil sonofabitch trying to take over."

"They trusted him. That disgusting bastard!" Miriam stands and marches for the door.

"No!" I rush to stop her, but she knees me in a strategic spot. I grunt and fall forward, the pain too crippling to move. *I can't believe she nailed me in the coconuts...*

"Hey!" I hear Miriam yell. "Clive! You out here?"

Oh God. I pry myself up off the floor and stagger outside onto the porch.

I can smell them in the air. Twenty, maybe twenty-five vampires. *And Clive...*

His tall frame emerges from the shadows. He is a man with plain looks—shaggy dark hair and a scruffy beard—but his dark eyes always struck me as kind. Now I know better.

"Michael, seems you are already defeated," Clive says, sounding amused.

I press my hands to my groin, trying not to faint. I cannot believe she did that to me.

"Did you kill my parents? On my fucking birthday?" Miriam roars.

Whoa. I hadn't realized. No wonder she did not want to celebrate. She was too busy remembering what was taken from her.

Clive simply stares but doesn't reply. Meanwhile, I am entertaining fantasies of giving him a slow death—something along the lines of dripping melted dark chocolate on his forehead for a few weeks.

"Answer me, goddammit!" Miriam stomps her foot.

Clive nods cordially. "They were good people. But then again, so were all of my human allies."

"They were loyal to you," she says in a low, angry voice. "Generations of Murphys and I'm sure other families risked their lives to help you. They killed for you! And you repaid them with murder?"

"They were a mistake. My mistake. I had to correct it."

"You piece of pompous garbage," she growls. "I'm going to kill you." She rushes at him, and I manage to cut her off and shove myself between them.

"Let Miriam leave," I snarl at Clive, holding her back. "She is no danger to you. Just let her go, and you and I can settle this like men."

Clive laughs. "This is a new war with new rules, Michael. Honor codes and heroism are things of the past."

Before I can say another word, I am down on my back in the dirt. Clive has me pinned by the neck with his boot.

If I am going to dust here and now, then he is coming with me. I reach for his ankle, and just as he is about to swipe a hand at Miriam and I am about to remove his leg, a blur of white and black whizzes past.

I look up and Clive is gripping his throat. Red liquid is leaking out. "I...I..."

Poof!

I am suddenly covered in gray dust. *What the...?*

"Vanderhorsthsssth! You are a piss-poor *boobyguard. Choo* know that, yes?"

I hop to my feet. "Mr. Nice?"

He shakes his head of scraggly long black hair. "*Dat* man is a lunatic if he thinks I am giving up my so sexy love stories. Only happy humans can write those."

I hear struggles all around us in the dark forest. One man rushes at me, but I am too fast. He's relieved of his head before he has a chance to get anywhere near me.

Lula suddenly appears, and I raise my hands. I cannot imagine a more painful fight, but I do not have a choice.

"Back off, Lula. I do *not* want to hurt you."

She gives me a look like she doesn't know whether to laugh or tear my head off. "Oh. My. God! Michael!" She stomps her foot. "Are you ever, and I mean *ever* going to learn?" She throws her head back. "Jesus! Someone please teach this man how to trust!"

"Are you trying to tell me that you were not working with Clive?"

"Of course I was! So was Alex, you big fat bone-head." She points to a shadowy figure standing next to a tall pine tree.

Alex waves but keeps a safe distance.

Lula goes on, "How the hell else were we going to find out exactly who was in on all this? I mean…duh!"

"A little too convenient a story, Lula," I say.

"Hold on. You really don't believe me?" She points behind her. "Alex and I just killed all of the men waiting to take you out. And let us not forget that Clive's plan was absolutely ridiculous. He never could have won against fifteen thousand of us and seven billion humans. You of all people should be able to figure that one out."

"I did. I thought his plan was quite mad, but that did not mean he was not going to try to pull it off." I am also still unsure if Lula is telling the truth. "Or that you were not helping."

"Michael, seriously?" Lula huffs. "I put my ass on the line by pretending to be part of Clive's little coup. So did Alex. And we had to stick with it until we had every single name of the families, soldiers, and generals who've been helping him."

"Then why not tell me? Why keep me in the